Wind Chimes

Also by Jean Miller

The Island of Greasy Luck

Wind Chimes

Jean Miller

InspiringVoices®

A Service of **Guideposts**

ISBN: 978-1-4624-0447-6 (sc)
ISBN: 978-1-4624-0448-3 (e)

Library of Congress Control Number: 2012922690

Inspiring Voices books may be ordered through booksellers or by contacting:

Inspiring Voices
1663 Liberty Drive
Bloomington, IN 47403
www.inspiringvoices.com
1-(866) 697-5313

Printed in the United States of America

Inspiring Voices rev. date: 2/6/2013

In memory of my mother,
who encouraged me to write this book

Contents

Chapter 1

The Funeral

The funeral was over, and for the first time in her life, Maggie Tilford was alone. The death of her parents had come quickly—without warning. A second honeymoon to Hawaii had ended tragically for Jim and Margaret Tilford, when the plane in which they were traveling plummeted into the ocean.

The icy fingers of loneliness tugged at Maggie's heart as she sat by the living room window, staring blankly at the field beyond. Her lips touched the rim of a half-empty glass of Chardonnay. She consumed the contents, filled the glass again, and then sipped the wine slowly. She was mellowing, but the pain of loss and loneliness continued to gnaw at her. Would the emptiness ever go away? She knew there wasn't enough wine in the world that could erase her pain. Only God could mend her broken heart, but God seemed far away.

She hadn't felt the full impact of her loss until after the funeral, when friends and family departed, leaving her in the big empty farmhouse to grieve alone. She had no siblings or close relatives. The following Wednesday would be her twenty-third birthday, at which time she had planned to move from her parents' home and strike out on her own. She had saved enough money to buy a townhouse in the city near her work, but the death of her parents had changed all that. Now the farmhouse was hers——nine huge rooms and an attic. This wasn't in the original plan, but fate had dealt the cards. The house was old. The floors creaked, and the windows rattled when the wind blew across the meadow.

It's impossible to live here alone with all the memories, she thought, and the upkeep is beyond my capability. The situation was overwhelming, forcing her to take action. The sale of the house and property was imminent, and the sooner the better. She would begin by sorting through her parents' personal effects, and then choose the furniture she wanted to keep and auction off the rest. The acreage would be included with the sale of the house, 150 acres of rich Indiana farmland.

She rested her head on the back of her chair and closed her eyes. Outside the evening sun had disappeared below the tree line, and darkness was falling over the meadow. The bottle of wine was empty, and Maggie's eyes grew heavy. She was relaxed and ready for sleep. Wearily she rose from the chair, turned on the hall light, and slowly climbed the stairs to her bedroom. She left the door to her room partially open, allowing a trickle of light from the hallway to pass through.

Fatigue settled over her as she pulled on her pajamas and fell into bed. She snuggled beneath the patchwork quilt her mother had made from remnants of her childhood dresses. It was tattered from years of use, but it reminded her of her mother's love, and no matter how frayed it was, she would never part with it. Herman, the orange tabby, curled up beside her and purred contentedly. She gave him a gentle hug and then drifted off to sleep.

In a short time, however, she was awakened by the never-ending curse of loneliness. She sat up in bed. Her muscles ached, and dark shadows deepened under her tear-stained eyes. She thought about her parents, and she missed them. She struggled to put the nightmare of their death out of her mind, but the memory embedded itself into her brain like an incurable disease. She prayed for it to go away, but it wouldn't. She drifted in and out of fitful sleep for the remainder of the night. At daybreak, the light of the early morning sun filtering through her bedroom window awakened her. A gentle breeze floated through the lace curtains, lifting them gently away from the sill.

Herman swiped his soft paw across her cheek reminding her it was time for breakfast. Ordinarily he stayed in the barn, but, since she was alone, Maggie allowed him inside for company.

"Come on, old man," she said, swinging her legs over the side of the bed and rubbing her tired swollen eyes, "I'll get your food."

Wearily, Maggie followed Herman downstairs to the kitchen. Her heart ached when she passed the pine trestle table where she had shared many delicious home cooked meals with her mom and dad. Herman hopped up on the Hoosier cabinet where his food was stored, eying Maggie as she reached for a can of shrimp and tuna—his favorite. Herman purred with joy as she snapped the metal ring and pulled back the top of the tin. The aroma of its contents caused him to dance ecstatically in circles of anticipation. He engaged wholeheartedly, attacking the food as though he hadn't eaten in a week, and, in minutes, devoured it all. After eating, he washed his face by dipping his paws into his bowl of water, and then he ambled contentedly into the living room where he hopped up onto the sofa for a nap.

Unlike Herman, Maggie had no appetite. Sadly, the wine from the night before had left her with a slight headache, but after eating a piece of toast and drinking a cup of coffee, the headache subsided.

The tepid flow of the shower caused Maggie's tiredness to disappear, leaving her relaxed and refreshed. After stepping out of the shower, she slipped into a pair of faded jeans. As she pulled them over her hips, she noticed they afforded more room around her waist than usual. That came as no surprise since she hadn't eaten a square meal since the plane crash. Her petite frame couldn't afford to shed more weight without appearing anorexic.

The first order of the day was to sort through her parents' clothing, select the better items for charity, and discard the rest. Maggie took a deep breath as she opened the door to her mother's closet. It was neat and orderly, just like Margaret Tilford's life. Her dresses hung on plastic hangers and were arranged in categories according to use—dress, casual, and everyday.

Margaret Tilford had been a stately woman, plump, but not fat. Her best dresses were for church and an occasional night out. The casual dresses, mostly cotton print, she wore on shopping trips to town. Less expensive were the every day dresses she wore around the house, usually protected by an apron. The denim jeans and flannel shirts were for outside work. A farmer's wife didn't require a fancy wardrobe.

Jim Tilford possessed mostly work clothes; bibbed overalls, a denim jacket, and a pair of heavy work boots. For church, weddings, and funerals, he wore his black suit with a white shirt and tie, along with a ten-year-old pair of dress shoes. Maggie's father had been a robust man, six-feet tall and weighing 230 pounds. He was a jovial person and never had a cross word for anyone. He had been a deacon at the First Baptist Church for the past decade, and the community missed him.

Maggie finished boxing up her parents' personal effects by late afternoon. Herman woke up from his nap and expected a snack before his evening meal. As the cat lapped up a saucer of milk, Maggie sat at the kitchen table and drank a cup of warmed-over coffee left from breakfast.

While there was still light outside, she decided to explore the attic. She had no idea what she would find, if anything, because she was never been allowed to go there. A heavy padlock on the door had enforced the rule. Occasionally Maggie would question her parents about the secrecy, but their answer remained the same. "Nothing there would interest you, Maggie."

They gave no additional information, and she asked for none. However, there was no longer a restriction— her parents were gone. She was in control, and she was determined to see what was behind the door of the attic room.

She put her coffee cup in the sink along with Herman's empty bowl, and then climbed the stairs to the attic. She was mindful to act quickly because daylight was limited on the third floor. Hidden above the door lintel was the key to unlock the room. Her hand trembled as she placed the key into the lock. Slowly she pushed the door open. The room emitted a dank, musty smell that nearly bowled her over. At the gable end of the room was a small, round window where a long shadow of light trickled through. Hidden away in the room was a rattan table covered with stacks of old newspapers, a dress form with a fringed shawl draped over it, five fiddle back chairs, and a collection of family pictures in antique frames stacked against the bare studs of the wall.

Maggie stood surveying the room, questioning all the years of secrecy. Nothing looked out of the ordinary in this odd collection of antiquity. As she started to leave, she caught a glimpse of a barrel-top trunk half-hidden behind the chimney. She studied the object, debating whether to open it. Finally, curiosity got the best of her. She dropped to her knees and slowly lifted the heavy lid. Inside was a black silk dress, with a matching net overlay decorated with numerous tiny black beads. The dress was sleeveless, with a scooped neck and a dropped waistline. Beneath the dress was a matching beaded headband accented with a rhinestone pin. Although the dress was old, it was in good condition.

In the bottom of the trunk were old photos of people she didn't know. "Nothing of interest here," she mumbled. She was about to close the lid when a small velvet box caught her attention. It contained a gold, heart-shaped necklace. Beneath the box were three manila envelopes with a return address stating, *J.P. Witherspoon, 6 Bedford Place, Boston, Massachusetts.* The postmark on the envelopes was 1943. The first envelope contained a letter and three black and white photos of two little girls.

> *Dear Mr. and Mrs. Tilford,*
> *I'm pleased to inform you that all the necessary arrangments are complete pertaining to the matter we discussed recently. Everything seems to be running smoothly, and it should be only a few*

*days before the adoption is complete. I'm
enclosing some photos of the little girl
and her guardian, who is no longer able
to care for the child. Once the adoption
is complete, the records will be sealed
and unavailable for further reference. I
will contact you as soon as everything is
in order.*

Respectfully, J.P. Witherspoon

Maggie stiffened with surprise. Her hands began to shake as she thumbed through photos. The girls in the first photo wore long pigtails, dressed identically in striped coveralls, and were standing barefoot on a beach. The same children appeared in the second photo. One girl held a rag doll. In the third photo, the girls sat on a bench in a garden surrounded by flowers. Maggie studied each picture carefully, but they were faded with age, making it difficult to recognize much detail. She opened the second letter.

*Dear Mr. and Mrs Tilford,
I'm happy to inform you that the adoption
has gone though, and you can come to
Boston next week to sign the final papers
and get the little girl. She is six-years-
old and has suffered great emotional
trauma over the past year. Presently she
has lost all recollection of the past, but
someday her memory of the tragedy may
surface. In the meantime, I feel confident
that she will have a good home with you*

in Indiana. Please call my office and make an appointment to finalize this transaction.

Sincerely, J.P. Withersoon

Maggie's emotions ran out of control as she opened the third envelope. It revealed a well-guarded secret—DECREE OF ADOPTION.

Her eyes filled with tears. Anger replaced sadness.

"I'm adopted, and they never told me. That's why they didn't want me in the attic. I'm not Margaret Ann Tilford after all." She fell prostrate over the trunk and sobbed. "If I'm not Maggie Tilford, then who am I?"

Chapter 2

The Wedding

Detroit 1910

For months, the wedding of Detroit debutante Emily St. James to Joseph Martin Hilliard of Boston was the talk of Detroit's elite, and a generous amount of money made it the most noted event of the year. It was a formal affair attended by Detroit and Boston high society.

The daytime heat had mercifully dropped to a comfortable seventy-two degrees by dusk, and a refreshing breeze off Lake Erie drifted through the open windows of the chapel, where women fanned themselves with hand painted, foldable paper fans. Their perfectly groomed coiffure, buried beneath silk hats with wide brims, reflected starched sophistication.

The attire of Detroit's wealthiest socialites couldn't compare, however, to the beauty of the young bride.

Emily looked radiant in her white satin gown, with a pin-tucked bodice of handmade lace and standup collar. A simple crescent-shaped headdress of silk flowers with a fine tulle veil covered her auburn curls. The bride and groom made a striking couple—she in her princess-cut gown, and he in his gray cutaway coat and pinstripe trousers. After the ceremony, the couple hastened from the chapel, bidding farewell to their guests, rushing to the street where their new Model T Ford was parked.

Numerous young men from Detroit's wealthiest families had courted eighteen-year-old Emily St. James, but handsome Joe Hilliard had won her heart. The couple had met during the previous summer while their families were vacationing on a remote little island off the coast of Cape Cod.

The St. James family traditionally spent each summer at their cottage in Michigan's Upper Peninsula, but that year they vacationed on the East Coast because of a business conference Emily's father was required to attend in Boston.

The change wasn't in Emily's best interest, or so she thought. She argued she would miss her summer friends, biking around Mackinac Island, and sipping lemonade on the porch of the Grand Hotel. It was doomed to be a rotten summer, and no amount of persuasion from her parents could convince her otherwise.

None-the-less, her father insisted the change would do her good and broaden her horizons. So while Emily and her mother stayed in a rented seaside cottage on Nantucket, her father attended to business in Boston, joining Emily and her mother on the weekends.

"It will be a summer to remember," Randolph promised.

Randolph St. James grew up in Boston and married there. His plan was to settle in Boston permanently, but the growing automobile industry in Detroit lured him to the Midwest.

He was excited about the new method of mass production Ford had introduced. With more Ford cars coming off the assembly lines, the possibilities were endless in the future of auto making. Randolph wanted to be part of the action. He was an enterprising young man, and it wasn't long before he advanced in the industry, making all the right connections.

Emily was accustomed to money and all the things it could afford. She was an only child and wanted for nothing. Her home in Grosse Point was a sprawling Georgian Colonial situated off the main road, nestled among birch and pine trees. A brick drive led to the front entrance of the mansion, and another led to a carriage house where two black carriages were stored, but seldom used since the arrival of the automobile. The horses, Nell and Pat, also stayed in the carriage house, and when Emily and her friends weren't congregating around the swimming pool or tennis court, they took frequent rides on Pat and Nell around the grounds.

There was a garden party each year with Japanese lanterns strung across the veranda, lighting the evening sky with a dazzle of color. A caterer provided an endless amount of food and drink, while a band played jazz, and women wearing exotic costumes danced the Fox Trot. The annual garden party was usually held before the St. James family left for their summer vacation. This year, however, the garden gala had been postponed to autumn due to the trip East. This was just another factor fueling Emily's displeasure.

On the morning they were to leave for Boston, Emily was in a particularly bad mood. It began when her mother came to wake her just before daybreak.

"It's time to get up, Emily. Father has the car packed, and breakfast is on the table."

Emily rolled over and grunted.

"Get up, Emily. We have to get started. We've a long ride ahead."

She rolled on her back and looked up at her mother "I don't know why we have to go with Father to Boston. Can't we go to the cottage up north, and let Father go to Boston alone?"

"That wouldn't be fair to your father. He looks forward to our family vacations. I'm sure you'll have a good time once you're there. Just think of all the new friends you'll meet."

Emily realized there was no use arguing. She would rather die than go to Boston, but the sooner she got out of bed, the sooner she would be in Boston, and the sooner the summer would end—and then, she could come home and resume life as usual.

Chapter 3

The Appointment

Boston 1960

The discovery of her adoption changed Maggie Tilford's priorities. No longer was the sale of the farm at the top of her list, but finding her identity was. The only clue she had was the address of the attorney responsible for her adoption. Would she be able to contact him after so many years had passed? She had to try.

She dialed the telephone number on a business card attached to one of the letters, but the number wasn't in service. Refusing to give up, she called information and discovered that there was another listing by the same name but at a different address. With renewed hope, she dialed the number and spoke with a secretary.

"Hello, my name is Maggie Tilford," she said, "and I'm trying to locate Mr. J.P. Witherspoon. Is he employed in your firm?"

The voice on the other end replied, "Why yes, he's the senior partner."

"Was his office previously located at 6 Bedford Place?"

"Yes, that's right. He relocated ten years ago when Mr. Thacher and Mr. Kippington joined the firm. Why do you ask?"

"Its private matter regarding a case he handled several years ago."

"I see. What is the nature of the case?"

"I'd rather wait and discuss it with Mr. Witherspoon, if you don't mind." Maggie remembered the statement Witherspoon had made in his letter regarding the sealing of adoption records. If she revealed the nature of her business to the secretary, she feared he might refuse to meet with her.

"Well, in that case," replied the secretary stiffly, "you'll have to make an appointment."

"When is the earliest opening?"

"Mr. Witherspoon's schedule is filled until the first week of July."

"Aren't there any earlier openings?"

"I'm afraid not."

Maggie breathed a disappointed sigh. "Very well, give me the first available opening that week."

There was a short pause at the other end as the secretary scanned the appointment book. "He has an opening on July 2, at two o'clock."

"I'll take it," Maggie said.

"And what is your name again?"

"Margaret Ann Tilford, but everyone calls me Maggie."

"Very well, Miss. Tilford. You have an appointment on July 2, at two o'clock. If," she added, "you're unable to keep the appointment, please call twenty-four hours in advance."

"Don't worry, I'll be there," Maggie assured.

"Yes, well—we'll see you then. Good day."

"Good-bye," Maggie replied.

With the appointment three weeks away, Maggie had ample time to sell some household items, which would provide her with extra travel money. A neighbor agreed to take care of Herman and the house while she was away.

July 2, 1960

Maggie's bright blue eyes reflected tortured anxiety as she stood before the door leading into the offices of *Witherspoon, Thacher, and Kippington.*

She had traveled a long way to keep her appointment, and she hoped the attorney would remember her case and provide information about her family.

She moistened her lips, flipped a strand of blond hair from her eyes, and boldly opened the door. Her adrenalin peaked as she approached the desk of Amelia Lace.

"Hello," she said, in a strained voice. "My name is Maggie Tiford. I have a two o'clock appointment with Mr. Witherspoon."

Miss Lace glanced at her watch. "You're a bit early, Miss Tilford." The woman peered up at Maggie over a pair of wire frame glasses resting on the bridge of her nose.

"Yes," she agreed, "but I wasn't sure how long it would take to get here from the hotel."

"I see. Are you from out of town?"

"Yes. My home is in Indiana. I flew in this morning, and after checking in at the hotel, I came directly here."

"You must be tired from your flight. Take a seat. Mr. Witherspoon will be with you shortly."

The secretary's eyes trailed Maggie as she walked across the room and sank in a comfortable leather chair. She crossed her legs and nervously tapped the business card on the bend of her knee. Her stomach was in knots. Maggie hoped she had made the right decision coming to Boston. Life would have been much easier if she had never discovered the adoption, but she had chosen her path, and there was no turning back.

Five minutes passed. Maggie stopped the tapping and began tracing her fingers over the six miniature diamonds surrounding the face of her wristwatch. The watch was an early birthday gift from her parents two days before they left for Hawaii. It was an extravagant present, which she would keep for a lifetime.

A few minutes before two o'clock, a rotund, balding man darted from his office. "Miss Lace," he huffed, "cancel my appointments for the rest of the day. There's an emergency, and I must leave Boston immediately."

"But Mr. Witherspoon," the secretary sputtered, "Miss. Tilford is—"

"I'm sorry, Miss Lace. I can't wait for her. Reschedule her for later in the week."

"But Mr. Witherspoon, Miss. Tilford is here."

The attorney's cheeks flushed with embarrassment. "Oh…I see," he stammered, turning to face his bewildered client.

"I'm very sorry for the inconvenience, Miss Tilford, however, you see, I have to leave immediately. It's an emergency, you understand, and I simply can't see you today. I suggest you reschedule."

"Can't you spare a few minutes? I won't take much of your time. I've traveled a long way to meet with you, and I can't stay in Boston long."

Dan Kippington came to the elder attorney's rescue when he appeared in the doorway of an adjoining office. "If the lady doesn't mind changing council, I'm free until four o'clock today."

Dan Kippington was the youngest member of the firm. He had graduated from Amherst College, continuing his education at Harvard where he received his degree in law. His family roots dated back to early New England.

"That's an excellent idea," Witherspoon responded. "What do you say, Miss. Tilford. Do you mind if Mr. Kippington meets with you today?"

"I'm not sure," she faltered.

"Well, my dear, you haven't much choice," Witherspoon replied. "Either you see Mr. Kippington, or you must reschedule with me at a later date."

Maggie glowered at the senior attorney, shrugged her shoulders, and replied reluctantly, "I see. Very well, I guess I'll accept Mr. Kippington's offer."

Dan Kippington's office reflected the masculine scent of old wood and leather. Bookshelves reaching to the ceiling held volumes pertaining law and the classics. Maggie's eyes followed the young attorney as he stepped behind a massive walnut desk and settled into a plush executive chair. She stood opposite him feeling awkward and at loss for words. He studied her for a moment, and then extended his hand motioning for her to sit down in the chair across from him.

"How may I be of service to you, Miss. Tilford?"

Maggie balanced herself on the edge of the chair. "I'm looking for my parents, Mr. Kippington." Her voice cracked as she choked back the tears.

He looked puzzled. "If your parents are missing, perhaps you should seek the service of a detective."

"You don't understand. I'm trying to uncover the identity of my birth parents. You see, Mr. Witherspoon arranged my adoption with the Tilfords years ago. I came to Boston to speak with him, hoping he would give me information about my birth family. However," she added, with a note of disappointment, "I'm pleading my case to you instead."

The attorney shifted uneasily in his chair, "Ahem...I see. Well it does look like you're *stuck* with me, at least for today." He loosened his tie and leaned back in his chair, giving a condescending smile as if dealing with a temperamental child.

"Oh, please don't misunderstand. It was kind of you to offer your services."

"No need to apologize. I don't offend easily. Tell me, why did you wait this long to take action?"

"The Tilfords didn't tell me I was adopted. I found it out by accident."

"And how did that happen?"

"My adoptive parents were killed in a plane crash about a month ago. As I was sorting through their belongings, I discovered my adoption papers hidden away in a trunk." She blinked back the tears. "You can imagine my shock to suddenly realize I've been living a lie all these years."

"You never suspected you were adopted?"

"I didn't have a hint."

"Do you have the adoption papers with you?

Maggie reached into her oversized handbag and pulled out the large brown envelope containing the three letters from Witherspoon. She handed the information to the young attorney, and watched as he examined each letter carefully.

"According to this information, you were born in Boston. Do you reside here now?"

"No. My home is in Indiana.

"Where do you live in Indiana?"

"I grew up on a farm south of Terre Haute. My birth parents were very good to me, and I had a happy childhood."

"Then why not leave well enough alone. You could be in for a big disappointment. Birth parents don't always measure up to the standards their children envision. There are various reasons why children are adopted. Sometimes it's because they are orphaned, abandoned, or have unfit parents. Any of one of these situations can be devastating. You must also consider the legal fee. It can be expensive. Are you sure you want to go through with this? Is it worth the risk of disappointment? You've had a good home and a happy childhood. Isn't that enough?"

"No. I want to know about my birth family," she responded decidedly.

"Very well, I'll give this information to J.P. when he returns, and he can get in touch with you." He hesitated. "That is—unless you would like me to take your case. Mr. Witherspoon is a very busy man. It will take more time and money if he's involved."

"If you can help find my parents, then I don't object to you handling my case, Mr. Kippington."

"Excellent. I'll start working on it on it right away."

As Maggie started to leave, he asked, "Miss Tilford, have you had lunch today?"

"No, I haven't. In fact, I haven't eaten since last night. I was so keyed up about this meeting that I've had no appetite."

"Well, I haven't had lunch either, and I don't like eating alone. Will you join me? My next appointment isn't until four o'clock. There's a great little chowder house on the wharf just minutes from here. They serve the best New England clam chowder in Boston."

"Thank you, Mr. Kippington. I accept your offer."

"Please, call me Kip. Mr. Kippington sounds too formal. We'll be seeing a lot of each other over the next several days, so let's drop the formality."

"Then you must call me Maggie," she replied.

Ahab's Chowder House was located on the wharf overlooking the harbor. It was a small frame building covered with gray cedar shingles. A fishnet hung as decoration over one side of the restaurant, along with an assortment of wooden bobbers. Displayed in the front window were trays of sumptuous muffins—cranberry, blueberry and pumpkin.

"Those are the largest muffins I've ever seen," Maggie said, her mouth watering.

Kip chuckled. "Muffins are big in New England. No pun intended. I have one every morning for breakfast with a cup of black coffee."

The restaurant characterized the charm of New England with pine tables and captains' chairs, blue café curtains hanging on brass rods, and walls displaying primitive seascapes.

They chose a table by the window. "This is delightful," Maggie said, admiring the harbor view. "Back home I'm surrounded by cornfields."

"What do you do for a living?"

"I'm a teacher."

"You're school teacher? I suspected you were a model. If my teachers had looked anything like you, I wouldn't have played hooky so often."

"I can't imagine you playing hooky. You were probably at the top of your class," she purred, feeding his ego.

"I could have been, but sorry to say, I wasn't. In boarding school, I had my moments of rebellion."

"You went to a boarding school? I'm impressed."

"Oh yes, yes in deed. It wasn't so bad after I got used to it. I liked being on my own without Mummy or Daddy looking over my shoulder. I did my share of loafing, but it rarely paid off. I'll never forget the summer I had to remain at school to make up a couple of classes. It was agony missing a summer at our beach house on Nantucket."

"Do you mean the same Nantucket Herman Melville referred to in his book, *Moby Dick?*"

"Yes, Melville's Nantucket." There's only one Grey Lady."

"Grey Lady. Why do you refer to the island as the Grey Lady?"

"Because of the dense fog that frequently hovers over the island. It rolls inland over the sea, and, before you know it, engulfs the island. Sometimes it's so thick you can't see a foot in front of you. It smells good, too—salty like the sea."

Maggie envisioned the scene Kip had just described. She also pictured him jogging barefoot down the beach, wearing only a pair of khaki shorts, with the wind blowing wildly through his hair.

"A penny for your thoughts," he smiled

Her cheeks tuned scarlet. "Oh, I was just thinking

about my adoptive parents, and how much they would have enjoyed walking along the beach," she lied.

"Did you say that they died in a plane crash?"

"Yes. They were en route to Hawaii when their plane went down just before landing. I wouldn't be here talking to you today if they had made the trip safely, and my adoption would have remained a secret."

The time passed quickly and before they realized it, the clock on the wall struck four o'clock. "Sorry, I have to leave. I'm running late for my next appointment. Enjoy your lunch," he said, grabbing the check and taking one last sip of coffee. "Shall we meet tomorrow and discuss your case?"

"Yes. I'm anxious to get started."

"I don't have my schedule with me, but I'll call you tomorrow morning at your hotel. Where are you staying?"

"At the Harbor View Hotel," she replied.

Her eyes trailed him as he left the restaurant, then a cunning smile spread over her face. *I look forward to spending more time with him. What better excuse do I have, than to employ him as legal council? I believe Mr. Witherspoon did me a favor after all.*

That night as Maggie lay in bed, she thought about the strange turn of events that had led her to Dan Kippington. With his gorgeous face etched in her mind, she drifted off into a peaceful sleep—the first one in weeks.

Chapter 4

The Harbor View Hotel

Dan Kippington was suave and sophisticated. He had joined the firm of Witherspoon and Thacher after graduating from Harvard. He was tall, with a thick shock of sandy hair that fell lazily over his tanned forehead. His bedroom eyes could melt a woman's heart like butter. He could have any woman he desired, but his career came first, and although he had dated many attractive women, none had won his heart.

A broad smile crossed his face when Maggie appeared in the hotel lobby. She was attractive in a simple way, possessing a natural beauty that drew her to him like a magnet. He noted she walked with confidence— not intimidated by new surroundings. She was regal, but not snobbish. She was a combination of city and country rolled into one. He was partial to blond-haired women, and Maggie's soft bobbed hair was the color of flax bleached by the sun. She was wearing a navy blue cotton sundress trimmed in white piping, with a full skirt that hugged her slender waist, flowing gracefully as she walked.

"Good morning," he said. She smiled as he took her by the arm and guided her through the French doors leading into the dining room.

After they sat down, he asked, "Did you sleep well?"

She leaned forward and—with eyes sparkling—replied, "Fantastic! It was the best night's sleep I've had in weeks. I'm encouraged with the prospect of putting all the pieces of my life together. I have confidence in you."

"I hope I'll live up to your expectations, but don't give me credit too soon. We have a lot of investigating to do before we have all the answers. With the adoption records sealed, we have few clues to go on."

"Speaking of clues, I failed to mention the photos included with the letters. I brought them with me today. Perhaps they'll provide some help."

She took the photos from her purse and handed them to Kip. Maggie watched as he examined each one carefully. "What do you think," she asked.

"Do you recognize anyone in these pictures?"

"No," she replied.

"Does the background look familiar?"

"No, it doesn't."

"These photos represent a coastal setting similar to this area—perhaps the Cape or one of the islands. Obviously, they are of you before the adoption. Witherspoon alluded to that fact in one of his letters."

"But there are two children in the pictures, and they appear no more than four or five years old. Why didn't he send a photo of me at the age of my adoption?"

"Perhaps none was available." He was about to return the pictures to Maggie when he noticed two were stuck together. He struggled to separate the pictures, but they were fragile with age, and he was fearful of tearing them. "Do you have a nail file?"

Maggie took a pearl handle file from her handbag. She watched with curiosity as Kip slipped the point of the file between the upper left hand corners of the two photos. After prying the corners apart, he twisted the file around the edge of the pictures, working it toward the center. Once the file was in position, he moved it back and forth until the pictures separated.

A smile of triumph spread over his face. "Well, will you look at this? This may be our first clue."

An inscription was scrawled across the left hand corner of the photo—*Nan and girls, Summer 1942*. In the photograph were the same two children standing beside an older woman. Clusters of beach grass, a lighthouse, and a row of windswept cottages were in the background.

"At least we have a name, but the *real* identity of the woman and the girls is still a mystery." He took closer look at the lighthouse in the background. "This is the lighthouse at Brant Point on Nantucket! I'd recognize it anywhere. Perhaps someone on the island will be able to identify the people in these photos."

Maggie's eyes glistened with hope. "Do you really think so, Kip?"

"It's worth looking into. I suggest we go there and see what information we can find. How do you feel about spending a few days on Nantucket?"

"I'll do anything to help locate my family," she said.

"Then it's settled. I have a friend who is an innkeeper. I'll call and make reservations for this weekend."

Chapter 5

Boston

1910

*A*fter their wedding, Joe and Emily moved to the Back Bay area of Boston, where they settled into a two-story townhouse on Marlborough Street. The home was less pretentious than Emily's girlhood home in Detroit, but it was still upscale and catered to Boston's upper class.

The house was a wedding gift from the groom's parents. It was located in a quiet picturesque neighborhood, where Elms arched over brick sidewalks, wrought iron fences sheltered front gardens, and where gaslights lined the streets.

They were excited about Joe's new appointment in the School of Business at Harvard University. Their new Model T Ford provided daily transportation across the Charles River to the campus at Cambridge.

Automobiles were still a novelty that turned heads, and Joe was proud to be on the cutting edge of progress.

Emily settled into married life with ease. Her time in a finishing school had prepared her to be a competent wife and homemaker. She was not without skills in the arts, however. She had shown promise in painting since childhood, and several of her early works adorned the home in Gross Pointe. Unfortunately, her duties as a professor's wife required most of her time, leaving little time for painting.

Once a week she held high tea in her parlor for the wives of other Harvard professors. She attended school functions and dinners with Joe when duty called. Emily didn't tire of her busy schedule, and, in fact, she adored her place in the academic world, fitting in as though she was made for it.

Professor Hilliard was proud of his beautiful wife. She illuminated a room with her presence, carrying herself with dignity, but without conceit. Her Midwest upbringing reflected in her warm, friendly smile, making everyone feel at ease.

Emily was no stranger to fashion, always dressing appropriately for the occasion. For afternoon tea, she wore her favorite—a pale blue silk tea gown with a scooped neckline and sleeves buttoned at the wrist. For dinner, she preferred satin and lace, with a tasteful piece of jewelry for accent. She styled her meticulously coifed auburn hair high on her head, with corkscrew tendrils framing her heart-shape face.

A year after they moved into the house on

Marlborough Street, Emily discovered she was pregnant. Joe and Emily converted an upstairs bedroom into a nursery, with an attached bedroom for their nanny, Molly McGlone.

Molly was Joe's cousin who lived in Ireland, and, although the two had never met, they had corresponded for months. Molly had expressed a desire to come to America, and the job offer from her cousin provided the opportunity. Although she would miss her home in Ireland, Molly was excited about sailing to America. Joe made the arrangements. She was scheduled to arrive in New York in early April. Joe planned to meet her when her ship, the *RMS Titanic*, docked in New York Harbor. Joe's promise of a home and employment gave Molly new hope for the future, and the *Titanic* was the "magic carpet" making it possible.

Chapter 6

Nantucket

1960

A cool breeze from the ocean tempered the summer air as Maggie and Kip left Hyannis on the Friday night ferry. From her seat by the window, Maggie watched the lights from the harbor fade, as the steamship *Nobska* drifted slowly from shore. The shrill sound of the steam whistle, plucked by an impetuous gust of wind, faded away into the night. The lights from the steamer sliced through the darkness, cutting a hoary path through the black water.

Maggie turned to Kip and asked, "What time will we arrive on Nantucket?"

"Our arrival time is ten-thirty. Would you like a cup of coffee?"

"Yes, thank you." Her eyes followed him until he disappeared through a door leading to the concession stand situated on the lower deck. She rested her head on the back of her seat and relaxed. She was excited about going to Nantucket, hoping the trip would shed some light on her past.

When Kip returned with the coffee, Maggie asked, "What time is your friend expecting us?"

He shifted uneasily. "Well—"he hesitated. "To tell you the truth, he isn't expecting us."

"What do you mean," she replied, giving him a puzzled look. "You said you were going to make reservations."

"I *did* call him, but the inn was booked. In fact, all the inns on the island were booked except one— the Seafarers Inn. It's in town, and it's a pretty nice place—except."

"What are you trying to say?"

"Well, there's a rumor that the place is haunted. It's nothing to be alarmed about."

"It's nothing to be alarmed about! We're booked at a haunted inn, and you tell me not to be *alarmed*? " She raised her voice, disturbing the passengers sitting nearby.

"Simmer down," Kip said, putting his hand on hers. "No one has actually *seen* the ghost."

"That makes me feel *so* much better," she snapped.

"You're over reacting. I'm sure it's only gossip, and even if it *is* true, many houses on Nantucket claim to be haunted—mostly by friendly spirits."

"A ghost is a ghost," she sniffed. "When we

reach Nantucket, I'm taking the next ferry back to Hyannis."

"You'll have to wait because this is the last sail tonight, and the next ferry doesn't leave until tomorrow morning."

"Well, that gives me little choice. I guess I'll have to stay at the Seafarers Inn tonight, but, mind you, I'm returning to the mainland on the first steamer tomorrow morning."

"I still say you're over reacting. I doubt the place is *really* haunted," he defended.

"Then why was it the only available place on the island?"

"It has just had some bad publicity, that's all. I wouldn't have told you if I'd known you would be so testy. I'm sure once you're on the island, your negative feelings will vanish."

"I doubt that," she scoffed.

"Nantucket is a magic place. The island has a way of casting a spell, and when that happens to you, you'll never want to leave."

"I'm certain I won't *fall* under any spell. I just want to get back to Boston, finish my business, and return to my quiet life in Indiana."

The remainder of the trip was spent in chilled silence, and it wasn't until the lights from Nantucket popped through the darkness that the silence was broken.

"There she is," exclaimed Kip, "the Grey Lady! Isn't she lovely?" He took Maggie by the arm. "Come on, let's go topside for a better view."

As the *Nobska* rounded Brant Point, lights from the harbor shimmered like polished jewels on smoke-gray velvet. Maggie saw the red glow from the beacon at Brant Point, and heard the mournful cry of the foghorn bellowing through the silvery mist. The *Nobska's* powerful engine groaned to a slow halt, as the ship glided into the slip at Steamboat Wharf.

The mist from the fog brushed softly across Maggie's face, and the gentle breeze lifted her hair away from her face. The smell of the ocean was everywhere. It was clean—cleaner than any air she had breathed, and she tasted the sea salt on her lips.

The melancholy cry of the foghorn melted into the solitude of the night, as their cab bounced slowly down the cobblestone street. Like watchful sentinels in the night, gaslights cast a heathery glow in the foggy mist. Soon the driver turned onto a side street and stopped in front of a dilapidated two-story house that hadn't seen a coat of paint in years. A rickety picket fence stretched across the front of a neglected flower garden. A quarter board sign hung askew over the entrance—Seafarers Inn.

Their arrival awakened a scrawny little man snoozing in a chair by the fireplace. "Oh, you must be Mr. Kippington and Miss Tilford. I've been waiting for you. I'm the innkeeper, Silas McQuaide."

He sauntered over to the front desk and opened the guest register. "Sign here."

Maggie stared at the blank page. "Are we the only guests this evening?"

"That's right, Missy. You and Mr. Kippington have the inn all to yourselves. You're in the *Captain Braddock* room, and Mr. Kippington is across the hall in the *Obadiah Gardner* room. I'll take cash in advance, and there are *no* refunds." His eyes reflected no warmth or congeniality as he held out his hand to collect his due.

The inn reeked with a stale odor, and the floorboards squeaked beneath them as the innkeeper led them up a narrow flight of stairs. The hall was in partial darkness, causing eerie shadows to bounce along the walls.

Maggie measured her surroundings with uneasiness. "How old is the inn?"

"It dates back to the whaling days," the innkeeper replied. "It was built in 1825 or there 'bout. It belonged to an old sea captain. Some folks claim the old cap'n still watches over the place." McQuaide's protruding eyes rolled upward. "Lurks in the attic, he does. Some claim they've heard his footsteps late at night, when the moon is full."

Goosebumps rose on Maggie's arms and up the back of her neck. "But that's just a rumor, isn't it?"

"It may be so—and may not. Old houses are full of night sounds. Who's to say where they come from?"

"Miss Tilford and I aren't concerned with island gossip," Kip interjected. "To my knowledge on one has been harmed by a Nantucket ghost."

The old man rolled his eyes up at Kip skeptically. "Think what you will."

There were four guest rooms on the second floor— two on either side of the hall.

The innkeeper set their luggage down and handed them each a key. "If either of you need anything, just call me on the house phone. I'll be close by," he said, with a twisted smile.

"Thank you, Mr. McQuaide, you've done quite enough for now," replied Kip.

After he disappeared down the stairs, Maggie commented, "Strange little man isn't he? If he tells that ghost story to all his guests, it's no wonder he hasn't much business."

"Don't let it get to you. The old guy just wanted to scare you."

"Well, he accomplished that."

"You'll feel better after a good night's sleep," Kip assured her.

In spite of the inn's macabre reputation, Maggie's room was cozy and inviting. A cheerful Paisley print decorated the walls, and crisp, white Pricilla curtains hung at the two windows facing Nantucket Sound. Between the windows was a worn maple table with two ladder-back chairs. On the opposite wall was a fireplace with a handmade mantel of rough pine. A life-like portrait of Captain Braddock hung over the mantel.

A sudden chill fell over Maggie as a gust of air riveted through an open window. She hastened to close it, pausing long enough to discover the moon waxing behind a veil of fog.

Warm sunlight streamed through Maggie's bedroom window the following morning. In the distance, sailboats bobbed in the harbor, while seagulls soared overhead, diving into the water in search of food. The scene was breathtaking, and her previous thoughts of leaving Nantucket disappeared.

She joined Kip on the sun porch for a continental breakfast. Although the general appearance of the Seafarers Inn was drab, there were some bright spots, and the sunroom was one of them. It was a small area adjacent to the parlor, surrounded by three walls of windows, where Boston ferns hung in clay pots. An eclectic collection of tables and chairs painted white decorated the room. The floor and walls were painted steel gray.

Kip's eyes brightened when he saw her. She looked rested and less tense than the night before, and her smile revealed that her first night on Nantucket had agreed with her.

He rose from his seat. "Good morning," he smiled, as he pulled a chair out for her. "May I get you a fruit cup with a muffin and coffee?"

"A muffin and fruit sounds great, but I prefer a cup of tea this morning."

"You seem in a better mood," he commented. "I trust that you had a good night's sleep, and that you weren't visited by the ghost of Captain Braddock."

"I slept very well, thank you. I'm sorry for my outburst last night. How could anything evil exist on such a beautiful island?"

A broad smile spread over Kip's face. "See, I told you. It's the magic of Nantucket."

"Well, I wouldn't go that far, but I have to admit this is an unusual place, and I would like to see more of it. Will you take me on a tour after breakfast?"

Maggie and Kip strolled down Orange Street, passing houses dating back to the days of whaling. Some were gray with white trim, and some were white with black trim. Many of the two-story homes had a "widow's walk" on the roof—a porch-like structure from which one could see for miles. When they reached Main Street, they headed toward the wharf, where a row of small shops resembling fishing shacks was located. They continued to walk until they came to a quaint, red building with a sign over the entrance—Harbor Light Bakery.

"Maggie, there's a special person I want you to meet," Kip said. "This lady makes the best donuts and muffins in town. Her name is Adele Merriman."

Adele Merriman had been the owner of the bakery for the four past decades. She was not a pretty woman. She concealed her obesity under a long, loose-fitting dress. A baseball cap angled to one side covered her steely gray hair, framing her leathery face of friendly wrinkles, however, she was well liked because of her jovial personality and friendly smile. Over the years, she had made many friends with the summer people from Boston and New York. Some of those families were special to her, and she looked forward to seeing them each year. The children loved her jolly smile and her delicious donuts and muffins. Each child had a favorite, and she catered to its desires.

The summer season was a happy time for Adele until the summer of '42. After the accident, nothing was the same. Over the years she managed to put the incident out of her mind—until the day Maggie Tilford walked into her bakery.

"My goodness, look who's here! Hello, Kip," she greeted.

"Adele! How's my favorite girl?"

"Oh go on now," she blushed. "You know how to charm an old woman." Then her eyes shifted to Maggie. "Who's your pretty friend?"

"I want you to meet Maggie Tilford. This is her first trip to Nantucket, and I couldn't think of a better way to introduce her to the island than by sampling one of your delicious blueberry donuts."

Adele's heart skipped a beat as she scrutinized Maggie. The young woman's eyes looked hauntingly familiar. This troubled Adele. Never the less, she forced a smile and said, "Well, I'm mighty glad to meet you, Maggie."

"I'm happy to meet you, Mrs. Merriman."

"Please, call me Adele," she said, then she touched her chin and gave Maggie an inquisitive look. "This is your *first* visit to Nantucket?"

"Yes, it is. It certainly is a magi—I mean," she stammered, "it's a beautiful island."

Adele repeated, "Are you sure you've *never* been here before?"

"Yes, I'm quite sure. Kip and I arrived last night on the ferry from Hyannis. We're staying at the Seafarers Inn."

"The inn operated by Silas McQuaide. Mmmm—he's a strange man. Are you staying long?"

"We're not sure," Kip replied, "we've some unfinished business that has brought us here. Maggie has employed me as her legal counselor regarding a personal matter."

Adele's suspicion mounted, but she tried to mask her uneasiness. "Well, enjoy your visit."

"We've a lot of sightseeing to do, but first how about a half dozen of your blueberry donuts." Kip looked at Maggie. "Do you like blueberry donuts?"

A pensive, far away look came to her eyes. "Actually," she faltered, "I'd rather have a beach plum donut topped with cream cheese icing."

Adel's face turned ashen. "My dear, I haven't made those donuts in years, not since—" she stopped with guarded silence.

"What do you mean?" Maggie asked.

"I meant nothing. I was just rambling. Why don't you try the blueberry donuts? They really are quite delicious."

Maggie apologized. "I'm sorry. I don't know what came over me. What is a beach plum anyway? I can't imagine why I requested it. Yes, blueberry will be fine."

When Kip attempted to pay for the bag of blueberry donuts, Adele said, "Never mind, Kip. This is my treat."

Chapter 7

The Discovery

When Maggie woke the next morning, she found a note under her door.

Dear Maggie,

J.P. called late last night. An urgent matter has developed, and I must go to Boston. I'm taking the early ferry, and I'll return as soon as possible. Please forgive me for not telling you in person, but because of the early hour, I didn't want to disturb you. In the meantime, enjoy Nantucket. I'm sorry to leave in a rush, but I had no other choice.

Sincerely,

Kip.

At first, she felt abandoned, but then she realized Kip wouldn't leave unless it was necessary. She folded the note and laid it on the dresser.

After breakfast, she took a leisurely walk downtown to do some shopping. She wanted a new outfit, but the prices were more than she was accustomed. In spite of that, she decided to indulge herself by purchasing a pair of khaki shorts, a knit shirt, a pair of sneakers and a baseball cap with *Nantucket* written across the front. Pleased with her choice, she paid the salesgirl, and then rushed back to the inn to change.

It was a picture-perfect day, with the morning sun hanging like an orange globe suspended in space, casting a reflection of shimmering gold upon the water. Patches of beach grass bowed gracefully in the gentle wind. As she walked along the beach, her feet settled deep into the sand, leaving a trail of prints behind. After a short time, she grew weary and sat down, hugging her knees to her chest. She fixed her eyes on the sea, and inhaled the fresh salt air. In the distance, the *Nobska* was approaching Brant Point bringing passengers from the mainland. Some waved to her, and she waved back.

After resting, she continued to walk down the beach, passing summer cottages where sailboats anchored at private docks. Further on, the beach began to narrow, and an unordinary silence prevailed then, from out of nowhere, came the distant sound of wind chimes. She followed the sound to a path leading away from the beach, and into a wooded area covered with craggy underbrush. The music became louder with each advancing step.

When she was about a quarter of a mile down the path, she discovered an abandoned house—a two-story Victorian with a wraparound porch. The house was shabby, pocketed against a backdrop of nature's death and decay. Yet, in spite of its condition, the house retained a certain amount of the charm. A heavy carpet of green moss covered brick walk leading the porch, where pink and white morning glories spiraled around the handrail. Ivy clung mercilessly to the weathered clapboards, while a trailing arbutus snaked its way along the crumbling brick foundation.

She took several photos before walking to the back of the house, where she discovered an abandoned garden. In the middle of the garden was a scrub oak. Hanging from one of its branches were the wind chimes—six hollow metal cylinders suspended from a piece of driftwood. The sound was mesmerizing. She sat down on the stone bench by the tree, closed her eyes, and listened. Objects flashed before her—a beach, a sailboat, and a rag doll. When she opened her eyes, they disappeared.

The beauty of the garden had been snuffed out by every kind of weed and nettle the island had to offer. Nature's power was evident everywhere. It was in every corner, and in every nook and cranny. The valiant struggle to overpower life was evident in the overwhelming, restless war of nature to take over the garden. For years, the relentless power struggle continued. Nature fought to survive, but death prevailed. A thin line of water and beach was barely visible through the overgrowth.

As she sat quietly, visualizing how the garden might

have looked in earlier days, an army of dark clouds began circling overhead, and the wind began to blow. A summer storm was brewing. She scurried back to the beach, dodging whitecaps as they charged toward the shore with angry momentum. Sailboats bounced like rubber balls in the water. The downpour came just as she reached the Harbor Light Bakery. She dashed into the shop just as a loud clap of thunder rumbled across the sky.

Adele Merriman expressed surprise when Maggie barged in. "Gracious child, you're soaked."

"Do you mind if I stay here until the rain stops?"

"No, of course not."

"Adele," Maggie said, "I'd like to talk to you about our conversation yesterday."

"Oh?"

"Yes. You were disturbed when I asked for a beach plum doughnut, and you mentioned an incident that had happened years ago, but you didn't finish your statement."

Adele shifted uneasily and cast a nervous glance out the window. "Oh my, the rain has stopped. You'll want to get back to the inn and get out of those wet clothes before you catch cold."

That evening Maggie ate dinner at the Lobster's Claw, a quaint little restaurant on Broad Street. Afterwards, she sat on a bench overlooking Nantucket Sound, enjoying the sunset until the sun disappeared below the horizon, and darkness eased its way over the water.

When she returned to the inn, she came face to face with Silas McQuaide. "Good evening, Miz Tilford," he hissed. "I haven't seen Mr. Kippington all day. Did he check out early without notifying me? There's no refund for early checkout."

"Mr. Kippington has been in a meeting all day. He won't be in until late." she replied, not revealing that Kip was off island.

"I see," he said, his eyes reflecting blatant disbelief. "Well, I was just curious. Surely, he wouldn't leave a pretty lady like you here alone."

"Don't be concerned about me. I'm just fine. Good night."

"Are you sure I can't get something for you. Perhaps—some tea?"

"No thank you."

"Well, if you're sure I can't get anything for you, I'll say good night."

McQuaide's presence left her uneasy. She charged up the stairs to her room, and bolted the door. Safely inside, she took a deep breath and whispered, "Kip, please hurry back."

Chapter 8

A Mysterious Assignment

When Kip arrived at the office, he found J.P.
Witherspoon thumbing through a stack of papers on his desk.

"Kip, my boy," he said, glancing up. "Sorry to interrupt your Nantucket weekend, but something has occurred that needs our immediate attention."

"What's up, Sir?"

"As you know, I was recently called to the bedside of an elderly client who has been hospitalized for a number of years in a mental facility outside of Boston."

"Was that the reason you canceled your appointment with Maggie Tilford the other day?"

"Yes, it was. You see, my client, who shall remain unnamed, suffered a mental breakdown after a family tragedy many years ago. Unable to cope with the situation, her mind shut down, refusing to remember what had happened. As a result, she has spent the past several years in an institution, living in her safe little world until recently. Now, for some unknown reason, her mind has cleared, and she has summoned me to settle a legal matter."

"I don't understand how this situation involves me," Kip confessed.

"It's a long story, Kip, and I'm not prepared to disclose any more information at this time. I need you to do some detective work."

"Detective work?"

"That's right. I want you to find her will."

"But, Sir," Kip argued, "I'm presently working on another case. Why not give this assignment to Thacher?"

"I'm afraid not. You see, my client is quite elderly. Although she is lucid at times, she continues to drift in and out of reality. Her physical health is failing, and she hasn't long to live."

"I still don't see why Thacher can't take the case."

"The woman has property on Nantucket, and if I'm unable to locate the missing will and any living relative before she dies, the estate will be auctioned off for back taxes. There's a will hidden some where on the Nantucket property. Moreover, you, my dear Kip, are better acquainted with Nantucket than Thacher. You must extend your stay on the island to search for the will. My client will pay all your expenses. I'm not suggesting you stop working on your current case, but this one must take priority."

Kip pondered the situation. Since there was suspicion of Maggie's past connection to Nantucket, it would be possible to work on both cases at the same time. "I'll get right on it, Sir."

The sky was clear blue, the sea was calm, and gulls were everywhere. A family of sandpipers bounced across the sand, searching for food washed in by the surf. When Maggie arrived at the trail leading to the abandoned house, a wave of apprehension gushed through her, as she stepped over the tangled weeds covering the pathway.

The house stood in a ray of sunlight, like a phoenix rising from the ashes. The scene was surreal—like a dream in which a foreboding sadness prevailed. Maggie wanted to go inside, but fear caused her to hesitate. She was trespassing, but the compelling desire to investigate persisted. A chilling question hit her like a bolt of lightening. Was the house calling her, urging her to come in? She felt like a fly caught in a spider's web. Finally, she surrendered, and tossed caution to the wind. She climbed the steps, forced the door open, and stepped inside. The putrid stench of the mold and mildew, an accumulation over the years, stung her nostrils. In the foyer, patches of plaster had fallen from the ceiling, leaving gapping holes of exposed lath and puddles of white plaster dust on the bare floor. She ventured into the parlor where sheets, yellow with age, covered a roomful of furniture. Curiously, Maggie peeked under one of the sheets, and discovered a red velvet Edwardian loveseat. At each end of the love-seat was a small walnut table with carved rosettes. Additional furniture included a pump organ—with a mirrored top and matching candle stands—a desk, two floral tufted chairs, and a library table. A worn Oriental rug covered the floor. The room had four long, narrow windows with half-moon tops. A louver shutter covered each window, allowing a thin ribbon of sunlight to seep into the room.

The focal point was the fireplace with a decorative oak mantel, over which, hung the portrait of beautiful young woman, wearing a white chiffon gown with a powder blue silk cummerbund. The neckline dipped, revealing a hint of her modest bosom, and around her neck was a single strand of pearls. Nestled in the mound of her auburn hair was a gold tiara set in miniature diamonds. In her hand was a single white rose.

Maggie pivoted the area, photographing it with her eyes. A sudden chill fell over her, sensing she wasn't alone. More disturbing, was the unexplained familiarity she felt about her surroundings. The growing uneasiness within her drove her back to the foyer, debating whether or not to continue.

She went to the front door and tried to open it, but it wouldn't budge. She tried a second time, and a third, but the door refused to open. The house held her prisoner. Completely unnerved, she paused, allowing her mind to clear while she gathered courage to proceed. After a few moments, she bolstered her spirit, and started up the stairway, fumbling her way through the darkness. The accumulation of dust on the handrail left a layer of grit on her hand, and the stairs creaked in rhythm with each advancing step. She felt her way along the wall, focusing on a circle of light shining through a stained glass window, from the second floor landing.

It was there, she discovered two bedrooms and an additional landing, where a gallery of photos lined the wall. The collection consisted of five black and white 8x10 photographs in simple wood frames. A layer of dust covering the glass made it difficult to see the images clearly. Her knees felt like Jello as she rubbed a circle of dust away from the first photo.

The picture was of a young woman, wearing a white blouse with cuffed sleeves tapered at the wrist, and a skirt that touched the top of her high button shoes. A straw hat concealed a bundle of hair piled high on her head. Her hand rested on the trunk of a large tree, and her head turned to the right, casting a pensive, faraway gaze into the distance. She was the same woman portrayed in the painting.

The woman appeared in the second photo, holding a little girl on her lap.

In the third picture, the little girl was holding the hand of another child about the same age. Both girls were standing barefoot in the sand, wearing matching sun suits, and holding a bucket of seashells. Both had blond hair. One had refined features, while the other, who was shorter, had a pug nose and freckles.

Mesmerized by the pictures, Maggie failed to

hear the faint roll of the thunder in the distance, and the sound of the wind whipping through the trees outside.

She moved to the fourth picture—a tall, handsome young man wearing a white tennis sweater and white trousers. His arm was around the waist of a woman slightly younger than himself. In her hand was a tennis racket, and although she had an athletic appearance, she maintained a feminine demeanor, with shoulder-length hair, wearing flared slacks and a halter-top. The couple was standing beside a sailboat.

At that moment, a crash of thunder rattled the windows. The sound was threatening. It was time to go. The final picture, separated from the rest, hung at the end of the hall. As Maggie approached it, a deafening clap of thunder shook the house, while jagged streaks of lightening bounced about with terrifying force. Seconds later the picture crashed to the floor, and glass scattered everywhere. Maggie knelt down and picked up the photo. It was the picture of a sailboat.

Another crash of thunder rattled the house down to its foundation. Maggie was terrified. She dropped the picture, and she dashed to the stairway. The lack of light made it difficult to find her way down to the first floor. Cautiously, she took one step at a time, holding onto the railing for support. When she was midway down the stairs, the front door opened, revealing the silhouette of a masculine figure.

Her heart jumped into her throat as she huddled close to the wall. The icy fingers of fear gripped her until she could hardly breathe. Maggie waited, frozen to the spot, as she watched the person disappear into another part of the house. When he was safely out of sight, she sprinted toward the door. Her escape was almost complete…until she felt a tight grip on her shoulder.

Chapter 9

Molly McGlone

April 1912

For Molly McGlone, the trip to America was, indeed, an adventure. Born of hard-working Irish parents, she had grown up and had lived in Queenstown her entire life. Her middle class heritage had instilled in her the value of good manners, patriotism, and respectability, however, her respectability—at present—was at risk. For this reason, she readily accepted the position of nanny for Joe and Emily's unborn child, a decision that would provide a new start in America.

It was a cold April morning as she huddled among the crowd of anxious passengers, burrowing deep into her long herringbone coat, pulling the fur collar close around her neck, awaiting the arrival of the *RMS Titanic*. A wave of melancholy washed over her as the mighty ship came in view, realizing she was about to leave her homeland forever.

A few of the *Titanic's* passengers stood on deck, braving the unpleasantly cold weather to catch a view of the Irish coast. Slowly the steamer glided inland, rounding Roche Point, where it dropped anchor two miles off shore.

Crowds had gathered from as far as Cork City, twenty miles away, to witness the arrival of the famous unsinkable phenomenon. Spellbound, Molly gazed at gigantic size of the multi-decked ship with its four stacks looming skyward. She had seen pictures, but they didn't do justice to the ship. It was unbelievably awesome.

After one-hundred and thirty passengers boarded the ship, a long blast from the ship's steam whistle signaled nearby crafts to clear the way. The *Titanic's* last stop was at the Daunt Lightship, dropping off the pilot before sailing out to the open sea, beginning the long voyage to America.

Molly stood on the deck, watching her homeland shrink in the distance, knowing she would never see Ireland again, but hopeful that a better life lay ahead in America. By nightfall, the Irish coast had completely disappeared from view, and ahead was the icy, hostile, water of the North Atlantic.

Molly was booked in Second Class. Her room was similar to those in First Class, but on a less grand scale. The Second Class consisted of six decks accessible by an elevator. It included a Smoking Room, a Library, and a Dining Room. The staircase leading down to the Dining Room, while not as ornate as the one in First Class was, however, spectacular.

She hadn't eaten since early morning, so she had worked up a hardy appetite by dinnertime. For the evening meal, she wore a pale mauve tea gown, covered by a finger-length satin jacket with pearl buttons. The jacket remained unbuttoned for comfort because of the growing bulge in her belly.

The Dining Room was filled with happy, chatty people who were thrilled to be passengers on the maiden voyage of the *RMS Titanic*. It was the ship of dreams, the largest sailing vessel made by man, unsinkable.

The spring of 1912 came early. The trim back gardens of the townhouses in Queenstown were alive with flowers—Daffodils, Tulips and Narcissus. The hedgerows were a vibrant green, and the cherry trees were in bloom. Molly caught herself thinking about her parents and her home in Queenstown. She would miss the splendor of her mother's garden, and the scent of her father's pipe. The McGlones were proud people. She intended no shame upon her parents, and leaving them was difficult and painful, but it was for the best.

Her parents were grateful for the offer made by the Hilliards, inviting Molly to come live with them in Boston. Molly needed a new start and new friends, a place where no one knew her past. She decided to create a story, a tragic one, in which her husband was killed in a hunting accident. Of course, there was no husband–and there never had been.

The same galley as in First Class prepared the food in Second Class, and it was excellent. The evening menu consisted of an entrée with a choice of roast beef or veal pie, accompanied by a succulent choice of vegetables, an assortment of fine wines, and sinfully rich desserts.

Molly struck up a conversation with an interesting young man who was sitting next to her. He was an artist who had spent the past year studying in Paris, discussing his work with art critic Leo Stein and his sister Gertrude. He had boarded the *Titanic* at Cherbourg, the ship's first port of call en route to New York City. He was a free thinker and a liberal, who openly expressed his displeasure over the growing problems with the labor unions and the job conditions of the working class. His paintings, he said, expressed the less glamorous aspects of everyday life in New York City. He planned to open a gallery in Greenwich Village, allowing other *Ash Can* realists like himself a place to display their art.

After dinner, Molly returned to her quarters, exhausted from the day's activity, and ready for a good night's sleep. Her conversation with the young artist had taken the edge off her homesickness, and had made for a pleasant evening. She had no desire for a shipboard romance, but a companion during the journey pleased her.

The celebration of Molly's twenty-seventh birthday

was bittersweet, an event that took place in the company of her fellow passengers. The young artist, who had been her companion during the past two days, ordered a birthday cake in her honor. It was served during dinner that evening. After dinner, he gave her a gift—a modest gold-plated heart necklace.

Overwhelmed by his thoughtfulness, she unashamedly allowed a tear to trickle down her cheek. "How kind of you," she said.

"Consider it a gift from a friend who wishes you happiness and a long life in America," he smiled.

Sunday, April 14, 1912

The *Titanic* was scheduled to arrive in New York the following day. Molly's journey had been pleasant, and, for the most part, uneventful. She was tired of the open sea, and the uncomfortably cold weather that had driven many of the passengers from the chilly decks to inside accommodations. She was anxious to see her new homeland, and to meet her cousin Joe and his wife Emily. She hoped that her condition wouldn't cause reproach. She reminded herself that she and Emily had something in common with the birth of a child. The only difference being, Emily's child would have a father, and hers would not.

Molly was accustomed to attending church services each Sunday, and was pleased to attend the Divine Service held by Captain Smith in the First Class Dinning Room at eleven o'clock that morning. After the closing hymn, *O God Our Help in Ages Past*, she joined her artist friend for a seafood buffet served in the Second Class Dining Room.

After lunch, she returned to her cabin to pack. Later that evening she attended the Hymn Sing in the Dining Room. Afterward she met her artist friend on the deck for the final time.

As they stood topside staring into the empty Atlantic, he commented, "This time tomorrow you'll be on your way to Boston and to your new life."

"And you'll be home in New York." she replied tenderly.

A brooding silence prevailed between them, as she fingered the heart-shaped necklace around her neck. "Thank you for being my friend," she said. "Because of you, this trip hasn't been as lonely as it might have been. I shall not forget your kindness."

As the sun began to sink into the water, the temperature dropped. Molly shivered and pulled the collar of her coat tight around her neck. "I think I'll return to my quarters," she said. "I still have some packing to do, and I want to get a good night's rest. Tomorrow is a big day for both of us."

"I will bid you good-bye, Molly McGlone, and may God bless." The young man leaned toward her, kissing her tenderly on the cheek. His eyes trailed her until she disappeared from sight, then he turned and gazed into the empty sea. A foreboding silence crept across the water, an uneasy quietness. The air was near freezing, a cold that penetrated to the bone, causing him to thrust his hands deep into the pockets of his coat. Lost in thought, he contemplated his future.

Once inside her warm cabin, Molly slipped into a flannel gown and prepared for bed. By the time she finished packing, it was nine o'clock. She wasn't tired so she decided to read for a while, hoping to become drowsy enough to sleep.

The sudden drop in temperature had driven most passengers from the deck, to quarters inside. Some, like Molly, retired for the night, while others returned to the Smoking Lounge for a friendly game of cards. By ten o'clock, the decks were void of all passengers, leaving only the crewmembers to brave the freezing thirty-one degree temperature and the ghost-like calm of the night.

Molly's eyes grew heavy, the book fell from her hand, and soon she was fast asleep. In a short time, the booming sound of the ship's bell echoing from the crow's nest shook her from her sleep, followed by an unexplained crunching sound on the starboard side of the ship. The gentle motion of the mattress on her bunk ceased, telling her that the ship had stopped.

There was an anxious tightness in her chest. She questioned the sudden silence of the engines, a silence interrupted by the expelling of steam from the *Titanic's* funnels. Presently she heard the sound of feet shuffling outside her door, and muffled voices of concerned passengers. At first, there was no immediate sense of concern, and even later when the announcement came that the Titanic had hit an ice burg, there was still no fear of danger. Several First and Second Class passengers gathered to watch a small group of Third Class passengers play games with chunks of ice that had landed on the deck.

Crewmembers minimized the seriousness of the matter, assuring passengers there was nothing of which to be concerned. The iceberg had long since drifted off into the darkness, but it was plain that a great amount of broken ice remained on the foreword Well Deck. Convinced that they were safe, many returned to their cabins, others retired to the common areas, while others—more skeptical—remained on deck. Molly returned to her cabin to escape the freezing temperature.

In the meantime Captain Smith assessed the extent of the damage, which revealed the ship was not *unsinkable*, in fact, it was taking on enormous amounts of seawater and, in a matter of a few hours, would be at the bottom of the Atlantic. He ordered the wireless operator to send out a call for assistance to ships in the area, and then he instructed the crew to get the passengers up on the Boat Deck.

A Second Class steward knocked on Molly's door. "Put on warm clothing and your lifebelt, Miss, and report to the Boat Deck." There was a sense of urgency in his voice.

Molly quickly slipped a dress over her nightgown, pulled wool stockings over her bare feet, and slipped into a pair of shoes. Hurriedly she grabbed her coat and scarf, and joined the others on the Boat Deck. In her haste, she left her valuables behind except for the heart-shaped necklace around her neck.

The mood on the Boat Deck was somber. Rockets illuminated the night sky, signaling that the ship was in distress. Swarms of crewmembers were removing the canvas covers from the lifeboats, clearing the lines and fitting cranks to the davits to lower the boats. Women and children crowded into the lifeboats, while husbands and fathers stayed behind. Molly huddled down into the lifeboat hugging herself to keep from shaking. She glanced up at the people who remained on deck, and—sadly—she realized their fate was sealed.

Chapter 10

Kip Returns

*M*aggie jumped. The intruder's touch startled her, and she was unable to move, paralyzed by fear. With all the courage she could muster, she swung around and faced him.

"Kip!" she screamed. "What are you doing here? I thought you were in Boston."

"I came back late last night." There was a cool edge to his voice. "I might ask you the same question. What are *you* doing here? Do you realize that you're trespassing on private property?"

Her face flushed with embarrassment, trying to think of an explanation. His condescending cross-examination angered her, but Maggie had to admit she didn't have a logical answer. "I was curious," was the best excuse she could give.

"Well as the saying goes, 'curiosity killed the cat,' " he replied sharply.

"You haven't explained why *you're* here, Mr. Kippington," she shot back.

"I have good reason, and we'll leave it at that." He took her firmly by the arm and escorted her out of the house.

They were angry with each other, and neither spoke a word until they reached the beach. It was Kip who broke the silence. "It looks like another beautiful day."

"It certainly wasn't a few minutes ago," she grumbled. "As I was about to leave the house, it began thundering as though we were in for another summer storm."

"It hasn't thundered all day. The sky has been clear as a bell."

"But I heard it," she argued. "It shook the house so hard that a picture fell from the wall."

"You must have imagined it. There hasn't been a cloud in the sky."

"I can assure you that it wasn't my imagination, Kip. Come back to the house and I'll prove it to you." He'd already scared her, angered her, and now he was calling her a liar. She was on her last nerve, and she was ready to challenge him to prove her point.

"Maggie you're making too much of this," he told her, trying to calm her. "Let's just forget the whole thing."

"Absolutely not," she exclaimed. "I insist that you come back with me, and then you'll know that I'm telling the truth."

Kip realized there was no point in arguing so, to appease her, he agreed. "Very well," he replied, but there was noticeable skepticism in his voice.

Maggie was confident she was right, and it would

give her great pleasure to prove Kip wrong. She would have the last laugh. He'd be sorry and apologize. Nevertheless, as they drew closer to the old house, her confidence began to waver. What would she say if Kip was right? She didn't want to end up with egg on her face. *Well, it's too late to back out, she told herself.*

A stony silence prevailed inside the house like the inside of a tomb. Neither spoke as they climbed the stairs. When they stood at the spot where the picture had fallen, Maggie's mouth flew open, and her eyes nearly dropped out of their sockets. There it was as big as life; the picture was intact and hanging securely on the wall. She couldn't believe her eyes. Kip said nothing, but his patronizing smirk said volumes. Had her imagination played tricks on her? She knew she wasn't delusional. She was certain she heard the thunder and saw the lightening, and the picture did—indeed—fall from the wall, but she wouldn't be able to convince Kip of that. She was humiliated, confused, and on the verge of tears. Her head throbbed and her cheeks burned bright red with embarrassment. Never the less, she insisted, "I know what I saw. I know what I heard."

"Well, it appears that you only *thought* you saw the picture fall to the floor and you only *thought* that you heard the thunder. I've had enough of this nonsense, Maggie. Admit you were wrong, and stop wasting my time."

She was beyond arguing with him, but the incident left her with the determination get to the root of the matter.

Chapter 11

Silas McQuaide

*T*he last person Adele wanted to see traipsing into her bakery was Silas McQuaide. He was a distaining little man, with secrets they shared—secrets she wanted to forget. His weekly visits to purchase baked goods came like clockwork, buying an abundance of merchandise beyond the amount he needed at the inn. She often wondered what he did with all the baked goods he purchased, but he was a steady customer, so she didn't pry.

Silas was weird. He had no close friends or family. He moved to the island shortly before the Great War, bought a small fishing boat, and earned his living as a fisherman. In 1940, he stopped fishing, turned his house into an inn, and became an innkeeper. It wasn't long before a steady stream of European visitors began arriving on island, and they stayed at the Seafarers Inn. They attracted little attention from the townspeople, maintained a low profile, spoke mostly German, and kept their visits short. This activity continued over the next year.

In 1942, German U-boat activity became a serious threat up and down the East Coast, resulting in a twenty-four hour coast watch on Nantucket. This service was performed by a group of local volunteers, who walked the beaches looking for U-boats hiding in Nantucket waters. The island was a perfect place for transporting spies to the mainland, and Silas McQuaide was not above suspicion as a contact. No one pursued the matter of his involvement, however, and business went on as usual.

By the end of the war, the tourist trade at the inn had diminished, and eventually attracted only a handful of weekend guests. McQuaide lived alone in a modest apartment in the basement of the inn, seldom leaving the premises except to shop for supplies. This was one of those occasions.

"Mornin', Miz Adele," he greeted in his usual nasal twang.

"Mornin', Silas. What can I do for you? The usual variety of baked goods, I presume."

"Not exactly, Adele," then he added, "I have a couple of *special* people at the inn, who require a *special* treat."

"They must be exceptional, Silas, I've never known you to give preference to any of your guests before. What do you want?"

"A dozen beach plum donuts. You know the ones, don't you?"

Adele stiffened in anger. "I stopped making those after the acc—" She stopped in mid-sentence. "How dare you make a joke of that!"

A smile of satisfaction spread across his ashen face, and his eyes filled with evil glee. "Surely you can take a joke. Where's your sense of humor."

Adele's eyes narrowed, glaring at McQuaide as though she would like to strangle him. "What cruel jest even from you, Silas. The past, is past."

The innkeeper returned with a surly grin, satisfied that he had struck a raw nerve. "I'm just trying to be a *good* host," he grinned. "Kippington's lady friend looks like someone who would enjoy one of your beach plum donuts, don't you think?"

"Why do you think that?"

"Oh, it's just a feeling I have. I've been watching her ever since they arrived. There's something suspicious about her. You might find it interesting to know that she took a long walk along the beach recently while Mr. Kippington was away."

"Why is that so unusual? There are plenty of beaches here. After all, this is an island."

"But she chose a *particular* beach, the one that leads out of town, down a deserted path, to a certain old house."

"Why would she do that? It's off the beaten path. Most off islanders would never suspect the house was there, much less stumble on to it. She's never been here before. She said so herself. It's just a coincidence, that's all."

A suspicious look came over him. "Maybe so, maybe not, but I say we keep an eye on her—and young Kippington."

"Don't make any trouble, Silas, there's been enough heartache."

Chapter 12

Cat and Mouse

*K*ip was preoccupied during breakfast, pondering how to break the news to Maggie about his new assignment. Of course, he planned to continue working on her case, but Witherspoon's client had priority. He stuffed the last bite of a blueberry donut into his mouth, and washed it down with a gulp of coffee.

Maggie, too, was deep in thought. She had decided to extend her stay on Nantucket to learn more about the old house. She was contemplating how to break the news to Kip without stirring up suspicion, and to avoid his caustic warning about trespassing on private property.

"Maggie, I have something to tell you regarding my recent visit to Boston," Kip began. He leaned forward in his chair and explained, "J.P. has assigned the case of an elderly client to me. This client has some unfinished business on Nantucket, and an investigation must be made before her estate can be settled. The woman is near death, so there is a sense of urgency to settle her case. I have to stay on island long enough to take care of the matter. At the same time, I'll continue to work on your case, but it will take longer than planned." He shifted nervously in his seat, then continued, "I know you're anxious to find closure. If you choose to return to Indiana before I'm able to finish your case, I will keep you updated on my progress by phone." He braced himself for her reaction, fearing she would be disappointed and annoyed by the delay, however, he was wrong. He had given her the perfect excuse to extend her stay on Nantucket as well.

"That's not a problem, Kip," she smiled. "I've enjoyed my brief time here, and—since I want to learn more about the island—I, too, will remain a little longer."

Kip was jolted by her decision. "Well, that's a surprise. I was sure you would be annoyed. Not only does your decision allow ample time for business, but it will give me time to get to know you better."

She laughed at the irony. "Kip, are you forgetting, I don't even *know* myself?"

"But you will, Maggie. I promise before we leave Nantucket, we will both know who you are." He reached over, and squeezed her hand reassuringly.

"I'm counting on that," she smiled, returning the squeeze.

"Of course, this won't be all business. We'll add some pleasure to the mix. There are many places on the island that I want to show you, and since we don't have a deadline, we'll see them all."

A broad smile spread across Maggie's face, like a cat who had just caught a mouse.

"I'll look forward to it," she purred. Then she added, "But, Kip, don't neglect your other responsibilities because of me. I can entertain myself." Maggie needed some time alone without Kip tagging along because she was on a mission, and Kip wasn't a part of it.

Chapter 13

The Arrival

New York City April 1912

 he night was cold and rainy when the *Carpathia* carrying the *Titanic* survivors arrived at New York Harbor. Most of the victims suffered from shock, keeping to themselves, clinging to the hope that their friends and family members had also escaped death.

In spite of the thunderstorm, thirty-thousand people, along with a fleet of tugboats, ferryboats, and yachts—led by a large tug carrying the mayor and several city commissioners—gathered at the Cunard Pier to greet the *Carpathia*.

When the ship came into view, the mayor's tug let loose with a piercing blast from its whistle. The rest of the boats followed suit. As the *Carpathia* steamed up the channel, the weather worsened with torrents of rain, continuous lightening, and rolling thunder. Reporters pushed their way through the crowd, flashing their cameras, ignoring the onlookers, who stood by weeping silently. It was a dramatic ending to the *Titanic* disaster.

The *Carpathia* steamed past the Cunard Pier, making its way to the White Star Dock where it stopped. A hush of reverence fell over the crowd, as crew members from the *Carpathia* lowered the *Titanic's* lifeboats—all that remained from the ill-fated ship—and returned them to their rightful place. After that, the *Carpathia* returned to the Cunard Pier and docked. The original passengers of the *Carpathia* disembarked first, then came the survivors from the *Titanic*. They were a sorry lot, weather beaten, and grief stricken.

Molly McGlone trailed behind the others, dodging reporters who tried to board the ship. Her flaxen hair was unkempt, hanging loosely around her shoulders, while a borrowed blanket covered her thin body, protecting her from the cold. She was a pathetic sight.

She stood on the gangplank scanning the crowd, searching for her cousin. They had never met, but she had a recent picture of him for identification. Clutching the blanket close around her, she strained in the semi-darkness, searching for someone who resembled Joe. The wind and rain dimmed her view, causing the faces in the crowd to blur. Finally, her eyes fell on a tall, handsome man standing under a large black umbrella, wearing a top hat and dark knee-length coat. She was certain the man was Joe. In an instant, she dropped the blanket, raced down the gangplank, and into his arms. Tears of happiness ran down her cheeks. She was safe at last.

"We were happy to receive news of your rescue, Cousin," he said. "You're home now. Emily is preparing your room, and she's anxious to meet you."

Molly's living space was located on the second floor. It consisted of a bedroom, a sitting room, and a nursery, making it convenient for her to care for both hers and Emily's baby.

In October, Molly gave birth to a healthy baby girl who she named Bridget, and a month later Dorie Hilliard was born. The girls grew up together, sharing the same room, toys, and love from the parents.

The family, which included Molly and Bridget, spent summer vacations on Nantucket. They all loved the island and eventually Joe and Emily purchased a home there. The house was a stately Victorian, situated off the beach, down a secluded path, leading into a partially wooded area. They hired a caretaker to cut the grass, tend the backyard flower garden, and do general maintenance. In the evenings, the clean, fresh smell of the sea wafted through the open windows, followed by the clanging of the buoys from the harbor, and the lonesome echo of the foghorn at Brant Point.

Bridget and Dorie spent endless hours playing on the beach, building sandcastles, wading in the water, and picking up seashells. Bridget was shorter than Dorie, with a pug nose and freckles. Her eyes were as blue as the sea, and her skin was the color of cream. Unlike Dorie, she was shy, and had a fear of water and of sailing. Never the less, in spite of their differences, the girls got along famously and loved each other like sisters.

Chapter 14

Jedekiah Good

*W*hile Kip searched for the will, Maggie was free to gather information regarding the old house. Through her investigation, she discovered that a man by the name of Jedekiah Good had once been caretaker of the property. He was an elderly man, living in one of the fishing shacks in 'Sconset. Because Jed Good was well known on Nantucket, it was easy to acquire directions to his house. Maggie rented a bike at the bicycle shop, then rode to 'Sconset to pay the old man a visit.

On the way, she passed fields of Scotch broom and heather. On the bluff stood Sankaty Light, a proud reminder of bygone days when brave mariners sailed out to sea in search of the sperm whale.

When she arrived at Jed's humble cottage, she parked her bike against the wobbly picket fence in front of the house. An eclectic assortment of clutter filled the yard—fishnets, bobbers, two small rowboats, and a stack of lobster traps. Ignoring the "beware of dog" sign nailed on the gatepost, she boldly walked up to the front door. She knocked softly at first, but when there was no response, she knocked harder. The intrusion woke a black and white cat, who was napping lazily on the front porch. It gave an angry YOWL and ran away.

Unable to get a response at the front door, Maggie walked to the back. Peeking through the screen door, she caught a glimpse of a sink filled with dirty dishes, and several empty food cans strewn about. A plate of stale biscuits was on a table, along with a half-empty glass of milk, but Jedekiah Good was nowhere in sight.

As Maggie turned to leave, a scruffy German shepherd charged around the corner, barking and showing his teeth. Maggie broke into a run, attempting to reach her bike before the dog caught up with her. In her haste, she stumbled over the stack of lobster traps, causing her to fall and sprain her ankle. The dog continued the pursuit and had almost caught up with her when a barefoot old man, wearing a grimy shirt and torn jeans appeared.

"Rigger," the old man snarled, "you get over here!"

The dog stopped barking, hung his head, and crawled under the house. The man stood silent and glared at Maggie. "Who are you?" he barked.

Maggie wasn't sure who she should fear most, the man or the dog.

"I'm Maggie Tilford," she stammered.

"I don't recollect that name," he snarled. "Do I know you?"

"No, you don't. I'm looking for Jedekiah Good. He used to be a caretaker for a family who owned a house down by Brant Point."

"Is that a fact? Well, you found him. I'm Jed Good. What's your business?"

"I'm looking for information about an abandoned house and the people who once lived there."

"Well now, that's quite a bit of information yer asking fer. What makes you think I know anything about that old house? Are you considering buying it?"

"I might consider purchasing the property, but I'd like to know more about it first. Someone told me that you were previously the caretaker of the property. Do you know the name of the owner?"

"Well, I don't know you and…"

"*You* don't know her, Jed, but *I* do."

The sound of a familiar voice made Maggie's heart to jump into her throat. When she turned around, Kip was walking toward her, with an angry look in his eyes. She was trapped. She had no choice but to remain sprawled on the ground, helpless and embarrassed, waiting for the inevitable confrontation

"Kip!" she sputtered. "What a surprise to see you here."

"Yes, isn't it," he replied coldly. "I thought you were staying town today."

"I decided to rent a bike and explore some outlying areas," she defended.

"Well, it looks like your *biking* is finished for the day. I'll take you *and* your bike back to town."

Under the circumstance, Maggie had to swallow her pride and humbly accept Kip's help. She watched helplessly as he picked up the bike and tossed it in the back of the jeep, then he picked her up and dropped her into the seat beside him.

As they drove away, Kip yelled back to Jed, "I'll get back with you later, Jed."

"What was that about?" Maggie asked.

"I stopped by earlier to visit with old Jed. I had just left, and as I was heading back to town, I saw you sitting in the middle of the yard, whimpering like a wounded pup. Why did you venture all this way? You could have chosen a shorter bike path closer to town."

"I just felt adventuresome, that's all. I stopped to ask for a drink of water and was attacked by that horrible dog." She hated the deception, but she couldn't tell Kip the truth.

"I suggest the next time you feel like an *adventure* that you stay in town. There's enough there to keep you occupied."

"Thank you for the advice," she bristled, "I'll keep that in mind."

"You do that."

When they arrived at the inn, Kip helped Maggie to her room, while Silas McQuaide crouched in the shadows, his malevolent eyes clouded with suspicion and mistrust.

Maggie spent the remainder of the day resting in her room, sitting in an easy chair with her leg propped up, reading a book. Kip gave her an ice bag for her swollen ankle, and then left for the afternoon.

He returned that evening wearing a pair of faded jeans, a baggy white knit shirt—with the sleeves pushed up to the elbows—and a pair of leather sandals. He was carrying a medium pepperoni pizza and a bottle of wine

"I figured you'd be hungry after your little *adventure* today," he said. All trace of admonition was gone from his face.

"As a matter of fact, I am," she replied. "This has been a long afternoon, but I curled up with a good book, and my ankle feels much better." She removed the ice bag revealing her ankle. "See, the swelling has gone down."

"I took the liberty of bringing a bottle of wine. It's a sweet wine made from Nantucket cranberries." He poured a glass and handed it to Maggie.

She lifted the glass to her lips, sipping the wine slowly, allowing it to reveal the natural smoothness of the fruit. After a couple of sips, she leaned her head back and closed her eyes. "This is what the doctor ordered," she sighed.

After they had eaten, they sat on the loveseat in front of the fireplace. Maggie propped her foot up on the coffee table, while Kip sat at an angle facing her, draping his arm on the back of the loveseat.

"I guess I was a little hard on you this afternoon,"

he said, "but I was surprised to find you at Jed's house. Why *were* you there?"

"I told you, I was out biking and stopped for a glass of water."

He looked at her skeptically, and asked, "Really?"

"Yes," she replied emphatically. "Don't you believe me?"

"Is there any reason why I shouldn't?"

She knew he was on to her little game, so she decided to tell the truth. "Yes, I suppose you do have reason not to believe me. I was at Jed's house today seeking information about the deserted house down by the beach. In talking with some of the locals, I discovered that he was once the caretaker there. He must know the owners of the property, and I just wanted to find out who they are." Leaning her head on his shoulder, she looked up at him pathetically, and said, "Don't be angry with me. It's been a long day, and I'm really exhausted."

"I'm not angry with you, Maggie. I haven't been completely honest with you either."

She pulled away and faced him. "You haven't?"

"No. The case assigned to me by J.P. also concerns the old house. His client, a resident in an asylum for the past several years, has finally regained her memory. Now she wants to settle her estate before she dies. There is some question about a missing will, and if the will isn't found the property will be lost."

"Are there heirs to the estate?"

"That's another mystery. She thinks there might be.

Not only am I to find the missing will, but also any heir that might exist."

"Why don't we work together? We have a common interest in the house and family," Maggie suggested.

"True enough, but Maggie, my interest is business, and I'm not clear what your interest is, other than idol curiosity."

"I can't explain it, but I know there's something special about that house, and I won't have peace until I have some answers. Maybe it's part of my past. I experience a strange sensation each time I go there. I know I'm not making much sense, but down deep in my heart, I know the house is trying to tell me something. Please, Kip, can't we work together on this?"

"If what you're saying is true," he replied, "I may not be working on two separate cases, but one of the same."

Chapter 15

Otto Von Kulow

Nantucket 1917

*I*n spite of the war, summer on Nantucket went on as usual for the Hilliard household. As far as Bridget and Dorie were concerned, nothing had changed. Sadly, that was not so with other families who had loved ones fighting the war in France.

High on a bluff in 'Sconset was a cottage with a clear view of the Atlantic, and in that cottage lived Adele Merriman. It had been her childhood home, and she had lived there all of her life.

Shortly before the Great War, Adele married Otto Von Kulow. He was from Germany and spoke with a thick German accent. No one knew his background, where he came from, or what he did for a living. He was secretive, and frequently took nightly walks along the beach. Otto was a strange, quiet man who rarely ventured far from home, but Adele and their small son, Karl, walked to town once a month for supplies. Adele guarded her conversation, being especially interested in current news regarding the war.

When asked about her husband, she merely shrugged and said, "Oh, he's fine." Sometimes there would be noticeable bruise marks on her arms. Otto no doubt inflicted them, but Adele never admitted it.

Little Karl was shy and stayed close to his mother, occasionally speaking to her in German, but she responded in English. He resembled his father, having blond hair, blue eyes, and a square chin.

One day, as Adele and Karl were walking home from a shopping trip, they met Emily, Bridget, and Dorie on the beach. As the two women exchanged conversation, Karl joined the girls picking up seashells. The women smiled approvingly as the children skipped barefoot in the sand.

"You should bring Karl to our house sometime for a visit. The girls have a wonderful time playing in the garden and running along the beach. It would be good for him to be with other children," Emily suggested.

Adele hung her head and replied, "I'm afraid his father wouldn't allow that, but thank you just the same. We had better go before Otto comes looking for us." She turned and called, "Come Karl, we must go." Before the little boy returned to his mother, he grabbed Bridget's hand and kissed her on the cheek.

"He needs to be with other children," Emily repeated. "All children need friends, and so do people."

Adele didn't respond, but the lonely look in her eyes revealed that she agreed.

When she and Karl returned home, Otto always questioned her about the news from town. "There's talk of spy activity along the coastline," she reported. "Residents claim seeing someone walking the beach at night with a lantern. It's feared someone is making contact with the enemy."

Otto never pursued the subject, but after the war, he took his son and sailed back to Germany. He had given Adele a choice—leave with them, or stay on Nantucket. When she chose to stay, he gave her money to buy her silence.

Chapter 16

The Dream

*I*t had been a long day. Maggie's visit with Jed Good was a stressful experience, which provided no helpful information. However, the situation did create an openness between her and Kip. As a result, they agreed to combine forces, and look for the will and the missing heir together. With the truce between them, she didn't have to sneak behind his back anymore.

After Kip left, Maggie fell into bed, engulfed in tides of weariness. She curled between crisp, clean sheets, breathing in the refreshing scent of the sea, drifting through the open window. Soon she was lulled to sleep by the quiet, methodic clanging of buoys, and the steam whistle from the *Nobska* arriving from the mainland.

In a short time, a dream appeared. She was walking barefoot down the beach at Brant Point. As she approached the path leading to the old house, the silhouette of a young couple appeared a short distance away. She ran toward them, but before she was close enough to see their faces, a monstrous wave appeared and washed them out to sea. They called to her, but she was unable to reach them. Heartbroken, she watched as they disappeared beneath the surface.

Maggie bolted upright in bed, drenched in a cold sweat. She got up and went to the bathroom for a cold glass of water. Unable to go back to sleep, she collapsed on the loveseat. She tried to put her mind at ease, but the dream continued to swim in her head.

The next day, Kip called. "Good morning. How's the ankle?"

"I feel much better. I took an aspirin before going to bed, and the pain is nearly gone."

"Will you have breakfast with me?"

"Yes, that sounds great! Just give me a few minutes to shower and dress."

"I'll meet you at the Yellow Bird Café on Center Street. You can't miss it. Look for a little yellow building with a blue and white stripe awning over the entrance," he said.

The Yellow Bird Café was a quaint eatery, small, with Eastern music playing softly in the background. Tropical flowers and exotic birds were painted on the walls. A diverse collection of tables and chairs painted bright pink filled the room. On each table was a brown earthen bowl filled with raw sugar. The menu offered herbal teas, various granolas with cream, fresh fruit, and an assortment of wholegrain breads.

While Kip waited for Maggie, he ordered a mug of fresh ground coffee with two teaspoonfuls of raw sugar. He was on his second cup of coffee when she arrived, her hair windblown, wearing sunglasses, and smelling of lilac.

"I'm sorry if I kept you waiting," she said, dropping into the chair across from him.

He leaned toward her, took her hand, and smiled, "It was worth the wait."

The moment was interrupted when a server with long, straight hair, and almond skin approached to take their order.

After the waitress left, Kip said, "I jogged to the deserted house early this morning to look for the will."

"Did you find anything?"

"As a matter of fact, someone had been there before me. The house had been ransacked, drawers were left open and papers strewn about. It gave me the creeps, but I stayed long enough take a better look at those photos hanging in the upstairs hallway. Since Jed was the caretaker, he might recognize the people in those pictures."

"Didn't Mr. Witherspoon give you any information about his client? It seems a strange request for you to search the house without knowing her name."

"He was very secretive about that and, for some reason, wants to keep it that way, at least for now."

"Why don't we take the pictures to Jed and ask if he can identify them," Maggie suggested.

"That sounds like a good idea. We'll collect them after we leave here."

When Kip and Maggie returned to the old house, they noticed the outside door slightly ajar.

"I'm sure I closed the door earlier," Kip said.

"Perhaps the wind blew it open."

"Perhaps," he replied, skeptically.

When they went inside, to their shocked amazement, the pictures were gone.

Maggie and Kip looked at each in disbelief.

"What do you make of that?" Kip exclaimed. "Someone was here after I left this morning, or," he added, "they were *still here* waiting for me to leave."

"I hope they aren't here now," Maggie said, with a shiver in her voice.

"I doubt they are, but let's go. I don't like the look of this."

Later that evening Kip and Maggie went out for dinner and dancing at the Jetties House, an upscale hotel near the beach. The dining room was aglow with candlelight, where happy couples engaged in intimate conversation. Kip asked Maggie to dance, and as he gathered her in his arms, the firmness of his body and the manly scent of his aftershave put Maggie in orbit. She forgot about the unexplained happenings at the old house, her adoption, the death of her adoptive parents, and all the other unpleasant issues in her life. She was living in the moment—a magic moment—as she and Kip spun gracefully around the dance floor. She closed her eyes and imagined they were alone in the room, lost in romantic dreams.

As for Kip, Maggie felt good to him too. He had longed for a chance to hold her close since their arrival on Nantucket, but had kept his distance due to professional ethics. Now he had an excuse to hold her this way, and he took full advantage of it.

The night went on, the magic never waning as they laughed, talked, danced, and drank Cranberry wine. When the last dance ended, they strolled along the wharf enjoying the starry night and the whisper of the water lapping at the shore. They sat on a wooden bench facing the harbor, and watched sailboats rock in their moorings beneath the radiance of a moonlit sky.

"Have you ever been sailing?" Maggie.

"No, I never have. Remember, I grew up in the middle of two cornfields."

"We can change that. Let's go sailing tomorrow. I'll rent a boat. It will be another *adventure* for you."

"Do you know how to sail?"

"Of course I do. As I told you, I spent all my summers here while growing up."

She hesitated. "I'm not sure I'm up to it."

"Don't be afraid. It'll be fun. I'm good at the helm."

"It does sound like fun," she admitted. "Okay, it's a date."

Silas McQuaide was nowhere in sight when they returned to the inn. Kip slipped the key into Maggie's door, but it was already unlocked.

"I'm sure I locked it before I left," Maggie said.

Kip walked into the room ahead of her and flipped on the light. They looked around, making sure nothing had been disturbed.

"Everything appears in order," Maggie said, but then her face clouded with uneasiness. "Shush...I just heard a noise coming from over there." She motioned toward the bathroom.

About that time, Silas McQuaide appeared carrying an armload of fresh towels.

"Evenin'," he said. "I was just changing the towels. It's the chambermaid's night off. Do you want a turn-down, Miz?"

"No, thank you," she replied. The thought of him touching her bedding made her cringe.

"Very well," he replied. "If you need anything, let me know."

Their eyes trailed him as he slithered out the door like a snake through grass.

"He really gives me the creeps," Maggie whispered.

Chapter 17

Changes

Nantucket 1918

*T*he Influenza epidemic in 1918 created panic and caused many deaths in America. Molly McGlone was one of its victims. After the death of her mother, Joe and Emily became Bridget's legal guardians. The transition was an easy one for six-year-old Bridget, and from that time on she and Dorie regarded themselves as *real* sisters.

They buried Molly in a little country cemetery just outside of Boston. A modest stone marked her grave. The inscription read: *1884-1918. Here lies Molly McGlone, beloved mother of Bridget.*

Molly came to America for a better life. She found it through the generosity of Joe and Emily Hilliard. Bridget was her pride and joy. She left the child no money,but a rich legacy of love, and a piece of jewelry concealed in a velvet box.

Dorie and Bridget grew into attractive young ladies. They continued to summer on Nantucket with Joe and Emily, partying with old friends and meeting new ones. Boys swarmed around the girls like bees to honey.

For her sixteenth birthday, the Professor bought Dorie a sailboat, which he named *The Doria*. Dorie became an avid sailor, and loved the sea, spending the summer days sailing with friends around the island. Bridget didn't share Dorie's love for sailing; in fact, she was fearful of the water and felt distaste for it.

Once in awhile, Professor Hilliard invited a student from Harvard to join the family for a weekend. In the summer of 1929, Jamison West arrived from Boston to spend a few days with Joe, Emily, and the girls. He was a few years older than Bridget and Dorie, six feet, slender build, with raven black hair parted in the middle, and compelling brown eyes. He resided in New York City where his father, a banker, dealt heavily in stocks. Jamison was destined to follow his father's example.

Dorie and Jamison were attracted to each other immediately, and they became inseparable. They took long walks on the beach, sailed, picnicked, and enjoyed each other's company. Bridget felt alone and deserted. This could have created a breach between the girls if it hadn't been for a chance meeting with a childhood friend at the ice cream shop in 'Sconset. After eleven years, Karl Von Kulow had returned from Germany to pay a brief visit to his mother, Adele Merriman. Although Bridget and Karl hadn't seen each other in years, some physical characteristics remained from childhood.

"Do I know you?" Karl asked, as he approached the table where Bridget was sitting.

"I think so. Are you Karl Von Kulow?"

"Yes, I am," he said. "Are you the little girl I kissed on the beach?"

Bridget blushed. "I'm afraid so."

"I thought as much. I'd recognize those freckles and pug nose anywhere."

She blushed even more. "I'm not sure how to take that."

"You may take it as a compliment. I dreamed of you for days after that. I hoped my mother would take me to your house for a visit, but she never did."

"You and your dad left Nantucket all of a sudden, and there were rumors that your father was a German spy during the war."

"My father took me back to Germany because it wasn't safe for him to remain in this country."

"Was he a spy?"

His brow furrowed, "It doesn't matter; it's in the past."

"I'm sorry. I hope I didn't offend you "

"No offence taken."

"Are you here to stay?"

"No. I'll be returning to Germany to finish my education in political science at the university."

Bridget's eyes dropped in disappointment. "I was hoping we might see more of each other," she said sadly.

"I'll be here for the summer. I'd like to spend more time with you, that is, if you want to."

"I'd like that very much!"

At the end of the summer, Karl sailed back to Germany, Bridget and the Hilliards returned to Boston, and Jamison returned to Harvard.

In October of that year, the stock market crashed, and Jamison's father, after losing all his wealth, committed suicide. Fortunately, he had set aside a separate trust fund for his only son, providing for his education. After the death of his father, Jamison became a frequent visitor at the Hilliard residence, both in Boston and Nantucket. In the spring of 1933, he proposed to Dorie. Emily and Joe were delighted with the match. That same year Karl graduated from the university and returned to America to propose to Bridget.

The following summer a double wedding took place at the Hilliard home on Nantucket. Emily planned the affair for weeks, compiling a guest list of friends from Boston and Nantucket, along with Jamison's relatives from New York. Adele Merriman attended, but kept a low profile. The years of separation between her and Karl had taken a toll on their relationship. Unfortunately, the German influence created by his father made closeness between mother and son difficult. She left immediately after the ceremony.

Dorie and Jamison bought a house in Boston, while Karl and Bridget stayed on Nantucket, renting a country cottage on the west side of the island. Joe and Emily continued to spend their summers on the island, and the rest of the family joined them when their schedule permitted.

Emily was thrilled when Dorie and Bridget's girls were born, spoiling them with expensive gifts. The girls loved the beach and the sounds from the ocean. When they said the clanging of the buoys reminded them of chimes, Professor Hilliard made a set of wind chimes and hung it in the garden. The little girls sat for hours listening to the music.

Several times a week, Emily took the children to the Harbor Light Bakery and bought them a special treat—a beach plum donut with cream cheese icing, which Adele made especially for them.

July 4, 1942 began like every other holiday on Nantucket, with parties, clambakes, and picnics, but by the end of the day the festive atmosphere turned to sadness, and the Hilliard household was never the same.

Chapter 18

Juckernuck

Streams of sunlight poured across the water, while a mild breeze tempered the air making the day perfect for sailing. Yet, in spite of the idyllic condition of the weather, Maggie's anxiety lingered. The vastness of the water made her fearful. She enjoyed a beachside view of the ocean, but being in the middle of it was a different matter entirely.

She was unaware that the treacherous shoals, shifting sandbars, and unpredictable currents around the island created a challenge for the most able seaman. Had she been aware of it, she would have opted *not* to go sailing.

She hoped that her new two-piece bathing suit, concealed under her shorts, wasn't too daring. It was on display in the window of a fashionable boutique the day before, and she couldn't resist buying it. With her heart pounding in anticipation, she slipped a canvas beach bag over her shoulder, then left to meet Kip at the wharf.

His eyes raked over her when she arrived, wearing her khaki shorts and white shirt, hanging loosely around her narrow hips. The sun brushed golden highlights in her hair, and tinted her smooth skin to the color of soft ginger.

"You made it!" he yelled from the deck of the boat. "I was afraid you might back out at the last minute."

"Don't think it didn't cross my mind."

"You've nothing to fear." He helped her into the boat, then said assuredly, "I know my way around these waters like the back of my hand. You're in for a great *adventure*."

"I've been hearing that word, *adventure*, and a lot lately, and some of my *adventures* haven't been too pleasant," she joked, recalling the recent bike ride to 'Sconset and the unnerving encounter with Jed's dog, Rigger.

"You'll enjoy this one," he promised, handing her a life jacket. "Put this on," he said, "it'll make you feel more secure—not that you'll need it. It's just a precaution."

Maggie donned the life jacket, then moved to the back of the sloop where she sat, fixing a death grip on the side of the boat as they cast off.

"Relax," Kip told her, as the sailboat glided gracefully out of the slip.

Her eyes followed the curve of the shoreline as they passed Brant Point, leaving the lighthouse in their wake.

Slowly the thin gray strip of cottages disappeared, and before them was the vastness of the sea. Taking Kip's advice, she leaned back and closed her eyes, allowing the soft ocean breeze to blow through her hair.

Within twenty minutes, another strip of land appeared—Tuckernuck.

"Does anyone live on this island?" she questioned.

"It's mostly desolate, except an old hermit, and a few summer residents."

Kip guided the sailboat to the edge of the beach, where it rested on a cushy bed of sand. They strolled along the shoreline barefoot, dodging gentle whitecaps lapping at the shore, searching for a suitable place to picnic. When they came to a salt-water inlet, they knew they had found the perfect spot.

While Kip spread a blanket over the sand, Maggie casually removed her shorts and shirt, revealing her fiery red two-piece bathing suit. Kip looked at her seductively, but quickly reminded himself that Maggie was his client, not his girlfriend. In spite of his professional ethics, however, the desire lingered.

"This is a perfect setting for a picnic, don't you agree?" he said, trying to refocus his thoughts.

"Yes." Maggie purred, "It's like having our own dining room overlooking the sea. It's so quiet and peaceful." She dropped down on her knees and looked out over the water.

Kip sat down beside her. "That's why people return year after year. It's another life here *and* on Nantucket.

Cares and concerns from the mainland seem to wash away. It's all part of the magic."

"I suppose you're right. I must admit, I haven't thought much about the farm since arriving on Nantucket. Another interest has taken over."

"Are you referring to the old house?"

"Yes, the old house. I just can't get it out of my mind."

"Well, suppose you forget about it for today, and enjoy our lunch, the ocean, and being together."

"I'll try my best," she replied, shading her eyes against the sun. "This is certainly a gorgeous day." She reached into her beach bag and took out the bottle of suntan lotion. "Here," she said, playfully tossing the bottle, "do you mind rubbing some of this on my back and shoulders?"

He watched with anticipation as she dropped the straps of her bathing suit. The touch of her skin ignited a burning fire within him. He took his time applying the lotion with long, deliberate strokes across her bare skin. When he finally finished, he replaced the cap and set the bottle down beside her. By this time, he was no longer able to resist. Without a word, he gently turned her around and pulled her close, allowing the heat of his body to course down hers. He kissed her on the forehead, then on her cheek, and finally he pressed his lips to hers—slowly, passionately. The touch of his kiss caused a delicious sensation within her. She fought for composure, but he held her tight, daring her to pull away.

"Maggie, Maggie, you're driving me crazy." he whispered.

"Please, Kip," she replied, forcing herself from his embrace. "Our relationship must remain strictly business. You're from a wealthy New England family, and I'm a simple country girl who doesn't even know *who* she is. I can't get involved with anyone until I know my identity."

Kip exhaled a long sigh. He sat back and thought about what she had just said. "You're right about one thing. As long as I'm your legal council, we can't get involved, but as for the other, money doesn't mean that much to me. The person inside is what really matters. After we discover your identity, I warn you, Maggie Tilford, I will capture your heart."

With the matter of romance temporarily settled, they delved into their lunch prepared by the chef at Cap'n Toby's consisting of sandwiches, chips, fruit, and soda.

"I could stay here forever," Maggie said, observing the panoramic view of sand and water. "And, as I stated before, it's so peaceful."

"It should be peaceful, considering the limited number of summer residents living here. There are no amenities either—stores, services, public support, electricity, or running water."

"Wow! That's primitive. It's like another world."

"Actually we're less than a half hour from Nantucket," Kip remarked, "but the people here consider Tuckernuck their own private space, and outsiders aren't encouraged to visit."

"Are we are trespassing?" asked Maggie.

"Not exactly," he smiled. "Let's just say that we're uninvited guests. While we're here, let's do some exploring."

Beyond the beach, was a wooded area where vegetation grew wild, and where vines twisted around trees. The macabre scene produced an atmosphere of mystery and intrigue.

"I have the strangest feeling someone is watching us," Maggie whispered.

"Maybe it's the old hermit," Kip joked.

"That's not funny. Let's go back to the beach."

"You've been listening to too many ghost stories and now you're spooked."

"The thought of ghosts never entered my mind until I came to Nantucket. Since my arrival, I've encountered a haunted inn, an old deserted house with secrets, a thunderstorm that didn't exist, pictures missing for no reason, and a disturbing nightmare. I think I have reason to be spooked."

In the middle of Maggie's rambling, Kip shouted, "Maggie! Look over there. I'm sure I saw something lurking behind that tree."

The hair on Maggie's neck raised, and goose bumps danced on her arms. With her heart pounding, she grabbed Kip. "What did you see?" she asked in terror.

With that, he let out an impish laugh. "Just kidding, Mags, just kidding!"

She whirled around and glared at him. "That's not

funny, and don't call me 'Mags.' Let's go back to the beach. I've had enough of your humor for one day." Her voice was stern, but inside she was mildly amused.

When Maggie and Kip returned to the beach, they were surprised to see that dark clouds had gathered overhead. The wind was picking up, and a storm was brewing. By the time they reached the mooring, the sailboat was rising in the swell. Kip lowered the sails and secured them to the mast.

Maggie's fear of sailing escalated as she watched the angry surf heaving enormous waves toward shore. Kip helped her onboard and shoved the life jacket into her hands, then took one for himself. Maggie sat rigid with her hands clinched in fear as Kip started the small motor.

"With a little luck we might be able to beat the storm back to Nantucket," he shouted, over the deafening bellow of the increasing wind.

They were a few yards from shore when the rain came, drenching them with torrents of water. A towering wave rose before the boat, pitching it high in the swell then dropping it like a downhill ride on a roller coaster.

Kip fought bravely to keep the boat on course as it thrashed about in the raging water. In spite of his effort, however, he was no match against the angry water. "It's no use!" he yelled. "We'll have to go back to Tuckernuck until the storm subsides."

He struggled to turn the boat around, but a militant wave spilling mountains of seawater onto the deck overpowered him. The blinding rain made visibility almost impossible. Kip tried to keep the boat on course as it struggled helplessly against the violent surf. His clothing stuck to him like a second layer of skin, and his wet hair fell over his eyes.

Maggie tried to keep her balance as the boat rocked back and forth. She, too, was drenched with seawater, leaving her cold and shivering.

The surging water overpowered the boat's small motor, and although Kip tried several times to start it, the effort proved useless. "We'll have to use the oars," he shouted, handing one to Maggie.

"I've never used one of these," she shouted back.

"You'll catch on quick. Just watch me."

As Kip began rowing, Maggie followed suit gripping the oar with all her might to keep it steady in the water.

"Look out," she screamed, as wave smashed into them, throwing Kip to the floor. Stunned, he struggled to his feet and continued rowing.

"Are you okay?" Maggie shouted.

"I'm fine. I was just caught off guard for a moment."

No sooner had he uttered the words, than another wave hit starboard. He lunged forward, and nearly lost his balance again. Maggie braced herself as the boat went out of control, spinning in circles. Menacing jaws of black water grabbed the hull, washing them overboard. Kip attempted to reach Maggie, who bounced like a rag doll from one crest to another.

The dark, murky water closed in, pulling her downward. She struggled to the surface, inhaling deep gulps of air before the water sucked her down again.

Again, she surfaced. "Kip!" she called in desperation.

"I'm coming, Maggie." He swam toward her and grabbed her lifejacket, dragging her to the overturned boat. "Take hold. This will keep you afloat. The wind is blowing us toward shore."

Maggie clung to the hull with all her might, but it was no use. Her strength gave way, and once again she was at the mercy of the sea. Squinting through the rain, she tried to catch a glimpse of land. As she struggled against a vortex of churning water, memories—buried in her subconscious—flashed before her. She kicked wildly to stay afloat, but her lifejacket was no match against the force of the sea. She was encased in a watery grave where small fish and bits of seaweed floated before her. Everything was going black, and death seemed eminent.

She had almost given up when she felt a hand touch hers, and she realized she wasn't alone. Someone was reaching out to her, grabbing her, holding her. A soothing peace swept over her, then she lost consciousness. The next thing she knew she was resting safely on the beach. Through bleary eyes, she saw a stranger bending over her. She reached out to him, and then everything went black again.

When she came to, she could hear Kip's trembling voice. "Maggie, Maggie! Thank God you're alive!"

"Kip?" she uttered weakly.

He cradled her in his arms. "Yes, it's me. You're safe now."

She fell limp in his embrace, looking like a half-drown pixie. He brushed the wet strands of hair from her face. "Thank God you're alive," he kept repeating.

She looked up at him with a faraway look in her eyes. A thin smile spread across her lips. Softly, she asked, "Can you hear them?"

"Hear what?"

"The wind chimes," she whispered.

"There are no wind chimes, Maggie, only the clanging of the buoys."

"I can hear them," she insisted.

"You must have taken a blow to your head," he replied, "you've been in and out of consciousness for awhile."

"What happened?

"The boat overturned in the storm. Don't you remember?"

Maggie's eyes opened a little wider. "I remember someone calling my name, but it wasn't my name. It was another name, but I can't remember what it was."

"There's no one else around. Try to rest and put this out of your mind. We'll talk later when you're more coherent."

"Someone was in the water with me. I could feel arms around me. The next thing I knew I was safe on the beach, and a man was bending over me. He must have saved my life."

"Don't talk any more. There will be plenty of time to discuss this once we're back on Nantucket. The worst of the storm is over, and the Coast Guard will be looking for us soon. We'll wait here until they come."

Chapter 19

Stranded

Kip and Maggie sat on the beach waiting for help, but when the Coast Guard failed to arrive by dusk, Kip made a decision. "It doesn't appear that we'll be rescued today, so we'd better look for shelter while there's still light."

"Do you mean we'll have to stay here overnight?"

"I'm afraid so. I'm sure the Coast Guard will be here tomorrow. Obviously, we can't stay on the beach. Perhaps we can find a cottage further inland occupied by a summer resident who'll take us in."

The night was settling in, and it became difficult to find their way through the woods. To make matters worse, a thin layer of fog rolled over them, shrouding the woodland in a gray haze.

As they ventured deeper into the woods, Maggie's eyes fell upon a shack half-hidden in the trees. "Kip, look over there."

Through the shadowed darkness, was a dilapidated one-room hut surrounded by an assortment of weeds and wild flowers. "That's not a typical Tuckernuck cottage," he said, as they cautiously approached the hovel. Years of wind and rain had weathered the shack. The front door consisted of three wide vertical planks, and secured horizontally at the top and bottom by two narrow ones. When they received no response to their knock, they ventured to the back and peeked through the window. No one was inside.

"We'll stay here," Kip announced. "Chances are, the occupant won't be back tonight, and we will leave at first light tomorrow."

"Who do you think lives here?" Maggie asked.

"It's hard to tell. It could be a fisherman's shack, or a weekend get away, or—"

"Or what else could it be?"

"Well, it's just a long shot, but maybe the old hermit lives here. At any rate, whoever lives here, isn't here now. I suggest we make use of it. Frankly," he added with resignation, "we don't have much choice."

Inside the shack was a crude stone fireplace, a pair of bunk beds, a table and two wooden crates used as chairs. Stored beneath the table was a box of canned goods, paper plates, cups and plastic tableware. An oil lamp, a half-eaten loaf of brown bread, a wedge of cheese, and a bottle of Merlot were on the table.

"At least we won't go hungry," Kip remarked.

Maggie looked at her surroundings with despair.

"This place gives me the creeps, and there's no telling what lives in those mattresses."

"Well whatever lives there, it will have to share its bed with us tonight."

"Please, let's go," Maggie urged.

"There's no where else to go unless you want to sleep on the beach, and it gets chilly at night even in July. This might not be the Ritz, but it has everything we need, so let's make the best of it."

She realized he was right, and she had to admit she was cold and hungry. "I suppose I can stand it for one night."

Kip located a box of matches and ignited the lamp, then he started a fire in the fireplace with scraps of kindling he found in the wood box.

The silvery darkness outside was ominous, but the warmth of the fire and the soft glow of the lamp made the room feel safe and cozy.

"After all the excitement today, I've worked up an appetite. Are you hungry, Maggie?"

"I suppose I could eat if my teeth would stop chattering," she replied.

"I suggest that you get out of your wet clothes and put them by the fire to dry. Here," he said, tossing an old army blanket from one of the bunks, "wrap yourself in this. It might look grungy, but at least it's dry and will keep you warm."

She looked at him and raised her brow.

"Don't worry," he said, "I won't peek. I'll step outside while you change."

When Kip returned, he prepared a meal of canned beans, cheese, bread, and a paper cup filled with wine.

In spite of the awkward situation, Maggie trusted Kip. The question was did she trust herself. He melted her with his smile, and he was even more handsome in the soft glow of lamplight. A hushed silence filled the air.

"It's amazing," Maggie said, scooping the last morsel of beans onto her fork with a portion of bread, "this food isn't bad. The occupant must have been here recently, don't you think?"

"I'm sure of it, the question is, where is he now?"

"And how soon will he be back? What explanation would we give for eating his food and trespassing on his property?" Maggie said with noted concern.

"I guess we'll just have to face that dilemma *if* it happens. I doubt the person is on the island at this moment. I don't think we've any thing to be concerned about. Like I said, we'll leave at first light, and go back to the beach where the Coast Guard can easily spot us. This time tomorrow we'll be back safe and sound on Nantucket."

Although Kip tried to encourage her, Maggie couldn't shake the feeling that someone was watching them.

Both were pensive as they sat before the fireplace, drinking the last of the wine, watching the dying embers smolder into a golden blush. Night was upon them, and the fog wrapped them in a hoary veil.

Each cast a longing look at the other, then—tired and exhausted—they fell into their separate beds. Soon they were sound asleep, serenaded by night sounds whispering softly through the pines, but unaware of the shadowed figure that lurked close by.

Maggie and Kip wakened the next morning rested and anxious to return to Nantucket. As she rose from her bunk, Maggie stumbled over a piece of gray, weather-beaten wood protruding from beneath the bed. The board measured around four feet by ten inches with the word *Doria* painted on it. Most of the original paint had chipped away, leaving a dull, windswept appearance.

"What do you suppose this is?" she asked.

"It looks like the quarter board from a boat. I suspect it washed inland after a shipwrecked. People collect driftwood and other objects from the ocean. This is just another example. It makes a good conversation piece."

"Aren't you curious as to where it came from, and, if it is part of a shipwreck, what happened to the people involved?"

"I'm sure it has a history, but there have been many shipwrecks around here over the years. This is just another one."

"If you were aware of the danger sailing in this area, why didn't you say so, Kip?"

"It wasn't necessary because I know these waters. I've sailed here many times without incident, but I can't help what Mother Nature stirs up. If it hadn't been for the storm yesterday, we would have made it back to Nantucket safely."

"Well, here we are, just the same," she replied.

"Yes, here we are, and if we continue this conversation, *here* is where we'll stay," he told her, shoving the piece of wood back under the bed.

Kip slipped two twenty-dollar bills under the oil lamp to cover the cost of the food they had eaten the night before, and then he went outside while Maggie dressed.

They arrived back at the beach just in time to see the sun peek over the horizon. The sight was breathtaking. Maggie had to admit she hadn't seen one equal to it—not even in Indiana.

Black-capped terns were nested in the sand, while some took flight in search of breakfast, their trim, white bodies a vivid contrast against the sky. Occasionally one would dive into the water, disappearing for a moment, and then reappearing with a small herring or sand eel clinched between its beaks.

Maggie's eyes stretched over the water, but nothing was on the horizon. "Do you see any sign of the Coast Guard?" she asked hopefully.

"I don't see anything yet."

"What if we're never found?"

"Don't be silly," Kip said. "Of course, they'll find us. It's just a matter of time."

The words had barely left his lips when they detected the sound of a boat's engine in the distance.

Presently, a small craft popped up on the horizon with an American flag whipping in the breeze.

Kip and Maggie jumped up and down waving their arms to attract attention. The boat approached slowly, manned by men in uniform. The man at the helm cut the engine, allowing the craft to drift closer to shore.

He called to them, "Are you in need of help?"

"Yes," Kip shouted. "We've been stranded and need passage back to Nantucket."

As the cutter neared the shore, a lifeboat splashed into the water with two men aboard. "Prepare to board ship," came a voice over the ship's speaker system.

Maggie and Kip stood at the water's edge until the lifeboat was within a few feet, then they waded into the shallow water and stepped aboard. When they were safely returned the ship, the captain took them below and gave them a steamy cup of fresh coffee.

"We'll have you back to Nantucket in no time." Then the captain asked, "We spotted a small craft capsized not far from here. Was that your sloop?"

"Yes," Kip replied. "We got caught in yesterday's storm while attempting to sail back to Nantucket. We got hit full force and overturned. We nearly lost our lives."

"There was concern when you failed to return the sailboat to the boat rental. The harbormaster suspected you had run into trouble. He filed a missing persons report early this morning."

"When no one came for us, we found a place to spend the night," Kip said.

"And where was that?" the captain asked.

"In an old shack back in the woods."

"Sounds like the hermit's place. Was he there?"

"No, not that we were aware of. The place was empty, but there was food and bedding available. Have you ever met the hermit?"

"No, and no one else has to my knowledge, but I think he exists. By the way," he commented, "that was quite a storm yesterday. Once in awhile we get a bad one like that. Your accident occurred in the same area where one happened years ago. Five people lost their lives—four adults and a little girl. Only one body was recovered. It was a woman."

The conversation was cut short with the resonance of the boat's whistle announcing their approach to Brant Point.

"We're back on Nantucket at last!" Maggie shouted with joy.

Kip took her arm and assisted her as they disembarked.

"There are papers for you to fill out regarding your accident," said the captain. "After that, you're free to go."

Chapter 20

The Warning

When they returned to the Seafarers Inn, Maggie went straight to her room. She couldn't wait to remove her soiled clothing, which reeked with the stench of seawater, and to take a hot shower. She let the water flow over her for several minutes, giving her muscles a chance to relax. How good it was to be clean again.

Kip spent the day downtown searching through old public records looking for information regarding the abandoned property. His effort paid off. The house belonged to Joseph and Emily Hilliard. Finally, he had something concrete to go on. He remained puzzled by Witherspoon's refusal to give him the facts in the first place. Whatever the reason, Kip had the information he needed in spite of Witherspoon's silence.

His next step was to learn more about Hilliard family. There were still many unanswered questions, and complicating the matter was Maggie's unsolicited involvement. Why was she so intrigued with the property? Was there a connection? Was it Déjà vu—an experience wherein a person feels connected to a situation or place of which they had no conscious memory? At first, he thought she was just being a snoop, but now he wasn't so sure. Too many unexplained events had occurred, and no one—not even Maggie—could explain why.

Back at the inn, Silas McQuaide was oozing with questions. "I heard that you and Miz Tilford had a little boating accident yesterday," he said, as Kip walked through the door.

"Well, word gets around fast." Kip responded, clearly annoyed by the innkeeper's presence.

"Yes, it does indeed. Adele told me about it this morning. She heard it from the harbormaster. No one was injured, I hope." An evil smirk spread cross his face, as he rubbed his hands together waiting for Kip's reply.

"No, no one was hurt, but it was a harrowing experience." As Kip started to leave, the innkeeper grabbed his arm.

"Where did you go?" he asked.

"We went to Tuckernuck for a picnic."

The old man grimaced. "You don't say. Well, those waters can be rather dangerous, even on a good day." He hesitated as thought measuring his words carefully. "It must have been miserable spending the night in the water while waiting to be rescued."

"We weren't in the water, Silas, we spent the night on Tuckernuck. When we realized we weren't going to make it back to Nantucket, we headed back to the island, but we capsized before we made land."

"Did you spend the night on the beach?"

"No, we found an old hut in the woods and stayed there for the night."

The innkeeper's nostrils flared and his face turned red. "I see. Was anyone around?"

"No. The hut was empty, but there was evidence someone had been there recently."

"I wouldn't be snooping around. There's talk of a hermit living on the island, and you don't want to mess with him." McQuaide's words came more as a warning than as a concern.

"I'll keep that in mind. By the way, Silas, you've been around for a while. Do you know anything about a family by the name of Hilliard? They owned property down by Brant Point."

The old man's face turned from beet red to an ashen gray. "Hilliard? No—no, can't say as I have."

"I just thought I'd ask."

Although McQuaide tried to mask his deceit, his eyes revealed he was lying.

Later that evening, Kip told Maggie about the information he uncovered regarding the abandoned property, and about his conversation with the inn-keeper. "I think McQuaide knows more than he's saying. There's something weird about that man. I'm sure he can't be trusted," Kip confided.

From her bedroom window, Maggie saw a galaxy of stars transform into sparkling jewels in the night sky. The lace curtains billowed with graceful rhythm as a mild breeze floated in from the sea.

She began reading *The Ghosts of Nantucket,* and it was after midnight before she turned off the light and fell asleep. She was wakened before daybreak by the sound of footsteps. She sat up in bed, and listened, but then the noise stopped. She took a deep breath and thought, *Perhaps it was my imagination.* She settled back into bed and closed her eyes. She began drifting back to sleep when the noise began again. This time she was sure something or someone was lurking in the attic just above her. She was scared to death. At first she wanted to run to Kip's room, but fear stopped her. She pulled the covers up over her head and prayed, "Please God make it go away." In a short time, the noise stopped, and she fell back into a restless sleep.

The next morning she found a note under her door. *Stay away from the old house*, it warned. The message was unsigned, and written in an unsteady hand. She crumpled the note and tossed it into the wastebasket. A hot flush of anger to raged within her, as Kip's knock came to her door.

"What's the matter with you?" he asked, noticing the seething fury in her eyes.

Maggie stomped over the wastebasket and retrieved the crumpled note. "I found this under my door this morning."

Kip read the note carefully. "This sounds like our friend, McQuaide."

"My thought exactly. I feel like giving him a piece of my mind."

"That wouldn't be wise. You don't know for sure that he's the one who wrote the note. If McQuaide did write it, you shouldn't give him the satisfaction of knowing it bothered you."

"The note isn't all that's bothering me. Last night I heard noises coming from the attic."

"Are you sure you didn't imagine it?"

"At first I thought I had, but when it happened a second time, I was sure the sound wasn't my mind playing tricks on me."

"Well, if it happens again, let me know immediately."

"Don't worry, I will."

That night as a full moon hung in the night sky, a dark sinister figure hovered in the room above her, waiting for Maggie to turn off her light. Confident she was asleep, he began his nightly prowl in the attic. The noise woke Maggie, and she sat on the edge of the bed, listening. The more she listened, the more apprehensive she became. Quietly she slipped on her robe and slippers, tiptoed across the hall, and knocked on Kip's door.

""What's wrong?" he asked half-awake.

"I heard the footsteps again. This time they were louder and sounded as though someone was trying to get into my room."

"How could anyone get into your room from the attic?"

"I don't know. Come over and listen for yourself."

When they returned to Maggie's room, the light was on. "That's strange. I didn't turn on the light before I left." Shear fright swept through her as her eyes fell on a trail of wet seaweed snaking its way from the fireplace to her bed.

"It's the ghost! It's the ghost!" she screamed.

"Calm down. Let's not jump to conclusions. I'm sure there's a logical explanation for this," Kip assured her. "Someone may have entered your room while you were out."

Kip and Maggie followed the wet trail of seaweed to the fireplace, where it stopped abruptly. They inspected the area, and discovered that one of the panels next to the fireplace was ajar. When Kip pulled on it, the panel opened, revealing a hidden flight of stairs.

"Maggie, we've found the access into your bedroom."

Chapter 21

Lost at Sea

July 4, 1942

Shortly after the attack on Pearl Harbor, German U-boats were on the prowl off the East Coast targeting merchant ships in American waters. As the mainland prepared for war, so did the people of Nantucket. Many sons and daughters enlisted, the Nantucket Red Cross was formed, U.S. Coast Guard stations appeared at several locations, including nearby Tuckernuck and Muskeget Islands. Men who were over the draft age joined the Coast Guard, volunteering their boats for service. Their assignment was to patrol the island waters at all times, in all weather armed with only a radio and a rifle.

Shades were pulled at dusk each evening, automobiles were driven with lights dimmed, coast watchers patrolled the perimeter of the island on foot around the clock, but—in spite of that—merchant ships were sunk right and left by the U-boats just a few miles off shore. The American way of life changed, stirring up more patriotism in the hearts of Americans than ever before.

On July 4, 1942, there was a gala celebration on Nantucket. Flags adorned every house, and every shop in town. There was a parade down Main Street, a band concert on the village green, family gatherings, and clambakes on the beach.

The Hilliard family gathered to celebrate the holiday. Both Jamison and Karl were draft age. Jamison talked of enlisting in the Navy because of his love for the sea, but Karl showed no interest in joining the military. This concerned Joe and Emily because of Karl's German background. His aloof behavior mirrored that of his father, as did his nightly strolls along the beach. Karl's father, Otto Von Kulow, had left Nantucket after WWI under a cloud of suspicion, and "the apple doesn't fall far from the tree," as the saying goes. Regardless, Joe and Emily gave Karl the benefit of the doubt for Bridget's sake.

Dorie and Bridget's family planned a day of sailing, leaving at mid-morning and returning by dusk to comply with the blackout curfew. Joe, who was on afternoon beach patrol, and Emily stayed behind.

The children were excited about the outing, but shortly before they were to sail, one of the girls complained of a tummy ache and had to stay home. From her bedroom window, the little girl waved good-bye as the sloop, *Doria*, disappeared on the horizon. When the sailboat was out of sight, she fell into bed, clutching a rag doll, and slept for most of the day.

By late afternoon, the sky turned an ominous gray, and the wind picked up. The wind chimes in the garden whipped about in an uncontrolled cadence. Awakened by the disturbance, the little girl ran downstairs and fell into Emily's arms. They sat on the front porch, huddled in the white wicker rocker, waiting for the *Doria* to return. Distraught, the little girl whimpered, "I want Mommy and Daddy."

Emily tried to console the child, but to no avail. Dusk came, and Emily, too, was concerned. It was dangerous to be on the sea after dark when the U-boats were likely to strike. Overcome with worry, Emily took the child's hand, and they walked to the beach. As they stood at the water's edge peering into the bleak horizon, Emily prayed that no harm would come to her family. Hot tears streamed down the little girl's cheeks, as she held the rag doll tightly in her arms. In the distance waves rolled, tossing walls of water into the air. There was no sign of the *Doria*.

Chapter 22

The Secret Room

*K*ip received a call from his senior partner, J.P. Witherspoon early the next morning. "Kip, you must come to Boston today. I have some facts to share with you regarding your assignment. Leave on the next ferry and plan to spend the whole day in the city."

"I'll be there as soon as possible, J.P."

Regretfully, the search for Maggie's *ghost* would have to wait until he returned. Maggie expressed disappointment for the delay, but she was willing to wait until they could go exploring together.

With Kip off island, Maggie had the entire day to herself. Eager to learn all she could about the old house, she went to the Athenaeum, where she read past issues of the *Inquirer and Mirror*, the island's oldest newspaper. Her interest peaked when she discovered the announcement of Dorie and Jamison's engagement, along with a photo of the nuptials. They were easily recognized as the same couple who appeared in one of the pictures hanging in the upstairs hallway back at the old house. At last, she knew who they were. Her heart raced with excitement, and Maggie couldn't wait to tell Kip the news.

The more she read, the more curious Maggie became, as she scanned through issues covering the 1930s and into the early years of WWII. The stories of German U-boat activity off the East Coast captivated her. She had no idea the country had been so vulnerable in the early months of the war.

Her heart took a jolt, however, when her eyes fell on an article appearing on the front page of a 1942 issue. The headline appeared in bold print— BOATING ACCIDENT TAKES THE LIVES OF FIVE PEOPLE. The article read: *The holiday ended tragically for two young couples and a child when their sloop, the Doria, capsized and sank 25 miles off the coast of Nantucket during a storm. There were no survivors.*

Maggie felt sick to her stomach. She rested her head on the table for a few moments before continuing. When her head cleared, and her stomach stopped churning, she read the following week's issue: BODY FOUND. *The Coast Guard retrieved the body of Doria West late Wednesday. West was one of the five victims in last week's boating accident off Tuckernuck Island. The fate of the remaining four people, which included a child, remains a mystery.*

Kip's meeting with Witherspoon was enlightening. He finally revealed the name of his client. Her name was Emily Hilliard.

"She's in ill health, Kip. I can't stress how important is for us to find the will and the missing heir," Witherspoon remarked gravely.

"Did she indicate an heir exists, J.P?"

"Yes, and the heir is a woman, but Emily hasn't divulged her name. I'm not certain she is able to recall it."

"How can Mrs. Hilliard identify the heir, if she can't remember her name?"

"I'm hoping she'll be able to recognize the woman if she comes face to face with her. The mind is a powerful force, it has the ability to deny the past, forget the past, and recall the past. The presence of the heir might jog her memory, but that remains to be seen." He leaned forward in his chair and asked, "Have you made any progress in the case so far, Kip?"

"Well Sir, I've done some sleuthing on my own, and I found out the name of your client."

Witherspoon tolerated the news with unchallenged acceptance. "I should have been up front with you from the beginning, Kip, but I didn't want to give too much information prematurely. You see, someone on the island is determined to get the property, and will stop at nothing to obtain it. I don't know what the reason is, but I admonish you to be on guard and watch your back."

"I appreciate the warning, and I assure you I'll be

cautious. Some "red flags" have already gone up. I'll keep you posted."

A haze of fog hung over the water during the return trip to Nantucket. Kip stood on the top deck, leaning on the rail peering into the dark placid water of Nantucket Sound. He was anxious to get back to Maggie and share his news, but—more importantly—he was excited to see what lay beyond the fireplace in Maggie's room.

A thin drizzle of rain began to fall as he disembarked. From Steamboat Wharf, he hailed a cab and went directly to the inn. The streets of downtown Nantucket were empty, except for a few stragglers rushing to get to their destination before the downpour. Flashes of light filled the sky, and a low roll of thunder rumbled in the distance. There was a malevolent force in the air, eerie, foreboding, and ghostly. His apprehension grew as he neared the Seafarers Inn, where a dismal light came from the parlor.

Kip went straight to Maggie's room and knocked on her door. Before he had a chance to speak, she pulled him inside.

"I have some exciting news to tell you." Her eyes sparkled with excitement.

"And I have some news, too," Kip said, "but before we talk, let's check out the hidden staircase. We'll talk later."

Kip walked over to the fireplace, opened the panel, and peeked inside. His eyes fell on a narrow flight of stairs behind the wall. A lantern hung at the foot of the stairs. He took it off the hook and lit it.

Outside, the thunder became louder, and the lightening flashed like jagged shards of glass across the sky. Maggie huddled close behind Kip as they squeezed through the narrow passage, slowly making their way up the steep flight of steps. The light from the lantern reflected their shadowy images along the wall. At the head of the stairs was a door leading into a tiny room.

"This is spooky," Maggie shuddered, her voice trembling.

"In the early days secret rooms were used to store smuggled goods from the Orient," Kip volunteered. He held the lantern upward casting light on rough timbers supporting the roof. The walls were unfinished with lath exposed. The flame from the lantern began to flicker and dim.

"Looks like we're running out of oil," he said. "We had better call it a night, and come back tomorrow when it's daylight."

When they returned to Maggie's room, Kip shoved the panel back in place. "No one would suspect there's a secret staircase behind this wall," he said.

"Do you think Silas McQuaide is responsible for the noise in the night, or do you think there really is a ghost?" Maggie asked.

"It's McQuaide, all right. He invented that ghost story to scare us. I'm certain that the ghost is as human as you and I. The question is, why all the mystery, and what does McQuaide have to do with it?"

"If it is Silas, how does he get into the attic without entering through my room?" Maggie asked.

"There has to be another entrance," Kip said. "We'll look for it tomorrow." He dropped down on the loveseat, and motioned for her to join him. He took a deep breath, and said, "Let me give you an update. Witherspoon has affirmed that the name of his client is Emily Hilliard. She's been in a home for the past several years due to a mental condition. Recently her memory returned, and she claims there is an heir to her property." He turned to her and asked, "What did you find out?"

"I spent the day at the library scouring through some old newspapers, and here's what I found." Maggie showed Kip photocopies of the newspaper articles. "These articles prove that the couple in one of the missing photos is Dorie and Jamison West. Sadly, they, along with three other people, were later killed in a boating accident."

"You're a good little sleuth, Mags. Now we're getting somewhere." He gave her an approving peck on the cheek and then started for the door. Sleep well tonight, because tomorrow we'll do some serious investigating."

When they returned to the secret room the next day, they found it less gloomy than it had appeared the night before. This was due, in part, because of outside light trickling in from a small square window. The room was situated directly over Maggie's bedroom, with a window facing the harbor. Cobwebs hung in hair-like strings from the bare rafters, and a thin layer of dust covered the floor. There was no furniture in the room except for a single mattress and a blanket laying on the floor

At first glance, the room held no significant interest until Kip discovered a small door concealing a crawl space. The passage was just wide enough for them to pass. It led to an adjoining room with an exit leading out to the second floor hallway.

"I believe we've discovered how the intruder got into your room," Kip said. "He entered this room from the second floor, went through the crawl space into the room above yours, then down the secret staircase, and into your bedroom."

"How clever," Maggie commented.

The second room was about the size as the first, but filled with debris of sordid variety—a pile of clothing tossed in a corner, and a crude wooden box bound with sturdy rope handle. When Kip opened the box, he gasped. Inside was a WWI German Maxim machine gun.

"This is beginning to get very interesting," said Kip, carefully lifting the gun from its resting place.

"How would a gun like this end up in an attic on Nantucket?" Maggie asked.

"It may have been left here by saboteurs who entered this country on a U-boat. Who knows? It's possible. The coast was a hot spot for spies during both World Wars."

"Silas McQuaide is looking more and more suspicious," Maggie said, with a satisfied smirk .

"He certainly is," Kip agreed, replacing the gun back into the case. When he sifted through the pile of clothing, he discovered two tan army uniforms, a pair of dungarees, a heavy brown overcoat, a pair of black combat boots, and an armband with a swastika.

"It looks like we've just added WWII to the mix." Kip expression darkened. "Do you know what this means, Maggie? We may have stumbled on to the hiding place for a ring of German spies."

"Does this have any connection to McQuaide's strange behavior toward us?"

"I can't answer that, but something is causing it. Several pieces of the puzzle don't fit."

Chapter 23

The Meeting

Kip and Maggie were within a few yards of the old house when they heard loud voices coming from the garden. They hid behind a clump of bushes, and listened.

"Are you certain you weren't followed?" One man growled.

"Of course I'm sure. What do you take me for, an idiot?"

"You must not be too smart. They're still here. I thought you said you could get rid of them."

"Is it my fault they don't scare easily?"

Maggie took a firm hold on her camera and adjusted the telephoto lens. Silently she and Kip drew closer. She aimed her camera at the two men and snapped their picture.

"It's Silas McQuaide," she said breathlessly."

"Can you make out who the other guy is?" Kip whispered.

"He looks a little familiar, but I can't place him."

"Let's move closer to hear what they're saying," Kip suggested.

They crept as close as they dared, then they hunkered close to the ground and eavesdropped on the conversation.

"Where did you park that inflatable tub you call a boat?"

"Don't worry, no one will find it. I hid it in a patch of beach grass. By the way, that inflatable tub, as you call it, made you plenty of money during the war."

"Stop living in the past. If we don't find that will or the jewels soon, our mission will be in vein.

"If everything had gone as planned, I wouldn't be living in a run down old shack in the middle of no where." The man growled in a thick German accent.

"I've taken care of you, haven't I? I've supplied you with food and provisions over the years. That old woman of yours gives me the evil eye every time I buy those muffins and donuts for you."

"You don't need to gripe about that. I deserve some luxury for my miserable existence. She has her faults, but she can bake, and that's the only thing I miss about her, but even Adele's donuts and muffins get a little long-in-the-tooth after awhile. I'm tired of waiting."

"Have patience."

With that, the larger man grabbed the other by the collar and snarled, *"My patience is running thin. It's been ten years since I came back, and we still haven't found the jewels!"*

"It's not my fault the Doria got caught in that storm, and every one drowned."

"No one knows that for sure. They recovered only one body—Dorie West."

"Face up to it, your son is dead. He died back in '42 with the rest of them."

"It was all their fault–Dorie and Jamison West. If they hadn't talked him into going sailing that day, he and the jewels would be in Germany today."

"Do you really think he would have left his wife and daughter after the war?"

"Yes, for the money and the der Fatherland. She was the connection that enabled him to carry out his assignment. She trusted him, loved him, and never questioned his loyalty to her and to this country."

"What about the Hilliards? Did they know what he was up to?"

"They may have suspected, but they kept their mouth shut."

A greedy determination filled Silas McQuaide's eyes. *"When old lady Hilliard dies, the house will go to her heirs, if there are any, that's why we must find the will and destroy it. Once we buy the property, the jewels will be ours."*

The other man disagreed. *"I say we concentrate on finding the jewels and forget the will. It might not even* exist. For all we know it might be just the babbling of a crazy old woman."

"That lawyer from Boston is too nosey for his own good," McQuaide snorted. "He asked me if I knew a family by the name of Hilliard."

"What did you tell him?"

"I told him I'd never heard of them."

"Why do you think he asked?"

"He's here to locate the will, I'd bet on it. He has a girl with him, too. Tilford is her name—Maggie Tilford. I haven't figured what part she plays in this, but she has an interest in this house. She comes here frequently."

"Do you suppose they know about the jewels?" the German asked.

"Perhaps, and there's another fact that bothers me."

"What's that?"

"What if there is an heir to the estate? There were two little girls, and only one was on the Doria that day. If the other girl is still alive—"

"If she's still alive, and we find her, she'll be eliminated. Tell me more about the Tilford woman."

"I just have a bad feeling about her. She's a snoop, for one thing, and she takes pictures of this house for another."

"How do you know that, Silas?"

"I slipped into her bedroom one night while she was away and took a roll of film from her camera. When I had it developed, the entire roll was taken of this property, inside and out."

"So that's what happened to my film," Maggie whispered to Kip.

"I tried the ghost routine on her, but so far it hasn't worked," Silas continued.

"Maybe you should try a little harder. Give her a real scare next time. Rough her up a little," the German suggested. "Even if she's just a snoop, snoops can be dangerous. What does she look like?"

"She's an attractive blond, average height, a little underweight, but good looking, none the less. She and that lawyer fellow went boating recently, and they nearly drowned in that storm. Their sailboat capsized in the same location where the Doria went down. The Coast Guard rescued them the next day."

The man's mouth dropped open. "So that's who they were! That's couple who stayed in my shack overnight. Earlier, I found her half-conscious on the beach. She looked like a goner, so I just left her there. Later I returned to the spot, and saw a man sitting with her. I went back into the woods to hide until dark. When I returned to my hut, the light from my window told me someone was in there. I had to sleep in the woods all night. The next day they left, leaving money for the food they had eaten."

"You are a stupid idiot! You had the perfect opportunity to get rid of them."

"Silas, how was I to know who they were?" he lashed back.

McQuaide's attention was diverted when a sudden, vigorous breeze pitched the wind chimes back and forth, causing them to make a loud clatter.

"Those infernal wind chimes," he complained.

"Silas, you're getting jumpy in your old age. I would love to continue this pleasant conversation, but I have to get back to my island retreat." His voice dripped with sarcasm.

Maggie and Kip didn't move a muscle until the two men were well out of sight. When they were sure the coast was clear, they dashed from their hiding place and hastily made their way inside the house.

Filtered sunlight seeped through the windows in the parlor, falling on the portrait of Emily Hilliard. Maggie looked at the painting with a renewed awareness, realizing the woman in the painting had once lived in the house. Emily's eyes seemed to be telling her to *search for the answers.* Her spirit filled the room with love, and Maggie no longer felt like a stranger. This revelation, however, didn't ease her fear of discovering the truth.

She stayed close to Kip as they started up the stairs leading to the rooms on the second floor. She hadn't been in this part of the house before, and being there made her apprehensive.

In the master bedroom was a massive walnut bed, with a headboard so high it nearly reached the ceiling. Across from the bed was a dresser with a white marble top and button boxes on either side, and next it was chair covered in faded floral chintz. Three long, narrow windows were covered by threadbare drapes hanging from tarnished brass rods.

In the clothes closet, a white chiffon dress hung on a wooden hanger. Attached to the dress was a powder blue cummerbund, the dress Emily wore in the painting. Maggie carefully took the dress from the hanger and held it close to her body. She felt as though she was cradled in Emily's arms.

They bypassed the second bedroom, and proceeded to the second landing where the hall of photos had been. Off the hallway was a room of diminutive in size, with a warm cozy ambiance, and where a wallpaper print of soft pink roses covered the walls. A pair of white wrought iron twin beds set side by side, with a small table in between. Toys were strewn about—a miniature wicker rocker, a table and chairs, a rocking horse, and a doll carriage in which rested a rag doll.

"According to Jed Good, two little girls lived here." Kip said. "It looks like this was their room."

The room became deathly still, then came the faint sound of the wind chimes. "*Yes, this was their room,*" whispered a small voice inside Maggie's head. As if in a trance, she walked over to the doll carriage and picked up the doll. "*Raggedy Maggie*" a voice whispered inside her head.

Kip, noticing Maggie's strange behavior, asked "Do you recognize this room, Maggie?"

She looked at him through glazed eyes, as blurred

images danced in her head. "I'm not sure. It seems like I've been here before." Maggie hugged the doll, and tears began to stream down her face.

"Maggie, what's wrong?"

"I don't know!" she screamed. She dropped the doll and ran to the door, but before she could escape, Kip stopped her.

"Let me go!" she pleaded.

"No, you're not leaving," he insisted. "Something about this room upsets you. What is it?"

"*Raggedy Maggie, Raggedy Maggie,*" the voice kept repeating. She knelt down and picked up the doll, cradling it in her arms as a mother would a child. "*Mommy and Daddy are gone. We have to find them,*" the voice whispered.

Maggie's sudden transformation baffled Kip. He grabbed her by the shoulders and shook her. "Maggie, what do you see?"

She looked up at him with a blank stare, then her ice blue eyes snapped back at attention. "I see you, Kip. What a silly question to ask." Without hesitation, she casually tossed the doll aside. "Let's go back to the inn. I've seen enough of this house for one day."

Later that day, Kip returned to the old house to continue his investigation. A room beneath the stairway served as a study. Along one wall was a bookshelf filled with college textbooks, fiction, and historic accounts of Nantucket. Some books had been pulled from the shelves and tossed on the floor. The drawers of the desk were open, and papers were thrown about. Obviously, it was the work of an intruder. Kip thumbed through the books at random, noting Professor Hilliard's handwritten notes scribbled in the margins.

Among the collection, half-hidden on the top shelf, was a leather three-ring binder—Professor Hilliard's journal. Kip scanned the pages, and realized it held a wealth of information regarding the Hilliard family. Excited about the discovery, he tucked it under his arm and rushed back to the inn.

That evening Kip and Maggie read excerpts from Professor Hilliard's journal.

June 23, 1920
Today Emily and I bought a lovely old Victorian home on Nantucket Island. It's located in the woods near the beach. Emily, the girls, and I love our summers on the island, and owning our home on Nantucket makes us feel as though we belong. Emily and the girls plan to spend the summer decorating the old place. Emily insists on furnishing the house with her mother's Victorian Rococo. Since the house is patterned after the Edwardian style, it seems a logical choice. The expense to move the furniture to the island will be costly, but worth it since Emily and I plan to retire here. It will also be a place for Dorie and Bridget to bring their families after they marry.

September 6, 1928
Labor Day weekend has past, and summer is officially over for our family. Tomorrow we sail back to Boston. Dorie and Bridget will miss their island friends, the beach, and the ocean. Dorie will especially miss sailing in her sloop the Doria. Emily was reluctant for our daughter to have her own sailboat, but I was able to convince her otherwise.

Christmas Eve 1930
We are spending Christmas on Nantucket. When we arrived earlier in the week, the ground was covered with fresh snow. Dorie likened the moors to a fairy wonderland. The wind from the ocean was bone chilling during our sleigh ride to Great Point, but we were comfortable huddled between warm wool blankets.

Upon our return, we enjoyed a steamy cup of hot chocolate, while warming ourselves before the fireplace in the parlor. The girls were tired and went to bed early, but Emily and I remained in the parlor, watching the last embers of the fire burn to a soft glow. The Christmas tree in the corner reaches to the ceiling and is laden with presents. The bleakness of winter brings a quiet solitude to the island. Tomorrow the girls will help Emily prepare the holiday meal.

Christmas Day 1930
Emily and the girls prepared a delicious dinner of roast duck, cranberry-orange sauce, wild rice dressing and steamed vegetables. For dessert, Emily prepared her special Christmas pudding with rum sauce.

Summer 1934
This is a special time for our family. Dorie and Bridget are getting married, and Emily is busy planning a double wedding here on Nantucket. Dorie is marrying a former student of mine—Jamison West from New York.

Bridget's fiancé is Karl Von Kulow, the son of Adele Merriman. Emily and I aren't pleased with Bridget's choice. Karl's father was suspected of aiding the Germans during WWI. He left the country and returned to Germany shortly after the war, taking young Karl with him. Never the less, because of our love for Bridget, we will graciously accept Karl into the family.

August 1934
The wedding was held in the garden. It was well attended with family and friends from the mainland, along with our friends here on the island. I felt sorry for Adele. She attended the ceremony, but left shortly thereafter. She and her son Karl have been estranged since her husband, Otto Von Kulow, took the boy to Germany.

There was a reception after the ceremony. It was a catered affair, served under a large blue and white stripe tent. The weather was perfect. Our Dorie wore a white lace full-length dress, and a wide-brim matching hat. Her bouquet consisted of flowers from our garden.

Bridget was beautiful in a white satin gown, wearing a crown of miniature white daises in her hair. She wore her mother's heart-shaped locket around her neck.

Of course, Emily cried.

Fall 1937
Bridget and Dorie each gave birth to baby girls. We have prepared a nursery for them in the small bedroom upstairs.

Fall 1940

I've decided to take a sabbatical and stay on Nantucket for the winter. Perhaps the tranquility will be a tonic and restore my strength. Emily is looking forward to Christmas. Our family will be together for the holiday. Emily has begun making Christmas decorations for the twelve-foot tree in the parlor. When she isn't busy making Christmas decorations, she is sewing gifts for the little girls. She just finished making a rag doll, which she named Raggedy Maggie. She is unde-cided which child will be the recipient.

July 3, 1942

Although our lives are clouded by war, we haven't allowed it to hinder our summer vacation. The war has stirred a great amount of patriotism on this little island. The people here faithfully assume a volunteer watch along the beaches for enemy submarines and aircraft. I took my turn at the airplane-spotting tower on Mill Hill last evening. It seems strange to see military personnel walking about the streets. Because of its location, Nantucket is considered an important post in our nation's defense. The beach patrol has a "ghost fleet" comprised of private schooner yachts, which have been taken over by the government. The boats sail around the shoals undetected because they have no engines. Not long ago the crew from a British freighter, torpedoed by a German submarine, appeared on the south shore. The men were in the water for about six days before they were finally rescued. They were put into quarantine under strict military guard. The poor chaps were a grim sight, having suffered from hunger and exposure.

July 4, 1942
Today Dorie and Bridget's family are going sailing, and will return by late afternoon for one of Emily's delicious lobster dinners.

The final entry.

Kip closed the journal, and looked at Maggie in silence. Both were deep in thought, absorbing the information they had just read.

"This has been a stellar day for information," he said. "Let's recap what we've learned so far. First, we know the mystery client is Emily Hilliard. The Hilliards bought the house in 1920. They had one daughter Dorie, and they were legal guardians of Bridget. Dorie married Jamison West, and Bridget married a German by the name of Karl Von Kulow, the estranged son of

Adele Merriman. Adele's husband Otto was suspected of being a German spy during WWI."

Kip's eyes lit up. "That might account for the WWI machine gun found in the attic, which would also connect Silas McQuaide to subversive activities."

"The Hilliards didn't trust Karl for some reason," Maggie added. "Perhaps he had something to do with the WWII German military clothing also in the attic. Could he have been a spy or a German sympathizer like his father?"

"Our suspicion of McQuaide is well founded. According to the conversation with the man he met at the old house, there is more at stake than just the will. Apparently stolen jewels are hidden on the property."

"We still don't know how the jewels got there, or who was responsible." Maggie said.

"Perhaps we do," Kip countered. "I'm sure the stranger is Otto Von Kulow, and he has returned to get jewels that were smuggled in from Germany during WWII, and his son Karl was the contact."

"But Karl was killed in 1942 while sailing on the *Doria*"

"That's right, Maggie, but suppose Karl had planned to return to Germany with the jewels after the war? Unfortunately, he died and the jewels remained hidden somewhere in the old house. Apparently no one knew the location except Karl."

"And the only ones who know that the jewels exist are Silas McQuaide and Otto Von Kulow."

"Bingo!" Kip shouted. "That's why Otto has lived

as a hermit on Tuckernuck, to avoid prosecution for spying. It also gives him access to the property, and allows him to look for the jewels."

"And who's his contact on Nantucket?"

"Silas McQuaide!" they both chimed in unison.

"Otto agreed to split the loot in exchange for McQuaide's help. Kip, no wonder Silas feels threatened by us. We could spoil the entire operation."

"We have to be very careful from now on. Silas has admitted the ghost of Captain Braddock is a ruse, he knows you frequent the house, and he has taken film from your camera. He also is concerned that you might be the surviving heir. I think it's time to set a trap for our innkeeper, and get to the bottom of all this."

Chapter 24

Setting the Trap

*K*ip brought the journal with him to breakfast the next morning, and he and Maggie discussed its contents over a cup of coffee. Just as they had hoped, Silas McQuaide was in the next room eavesdropping on their conversation.

"The journal contains some very interesting information about the Hilliard family," Kip began.

"Did it say anything about the will?"

(From this point on, much of the conversation was fabricated to trick the innkeeper.)

"Oh yes, and much more. It seems there's a treasure hidden in the house. The Professor stumbled onto it before he died, and he names the exact location where it's hidden. Keep the journal safe in your room tonight, Maggie, along with the roll of film that you took yesterday. I'll take the journal and the film to Boston tomorrow. The Hilliard estate will finally be settled, and the jewels confiscated and turned over to the authorities."

They heard shuffling coming from the parlor, then the sound of hurried footsteps going up the stairs. McQuaide had taken the bait. They gave him plenty of time to search through Maggie's room then, after a half hour passed, they returned to see what had transpired.

Just as Maggie suspected, the back of her camera was open, and the film was missing. Other items in the room were disturbed, and it was obvious that McQuaide had been looking for the journal.

"Maggie, why didn't you hide the camera?" Kip scolded "Now he's stolen the film you took yesterday. That could have been used as evidence against him, and prove that Otto Von Kulow has returned."

"Do you mean this film?" she asked, with a smug grin.

Kip's mouth flew open as she took the film from her pocket and held it under his nose. "The roll McQuaide has is *unexposed*. I'd like to see the look on his face when he discovers he's been tricked."

Kip gave her a hug. "You sly fox," he said.

That evening Kip and Maggie switched bedrooms. He was certain that Silas would make another *ghostly* visit to Maggie's room to look for the journal, and, with the noose getting tighter around McQuaide's neck, there was no telling what he might do. Kip laid the journal in plain view on the table beside the bed, then he crawled beneath the covers and waited.

The foghorn moaned in the night, warning of the thick fog rolling in over the water. The lighthouse at Brant Point was a silhouette, barely visible except for its red beacon filtering through the darkness. When the clock struck midnight, Kip heard footsteps descending the stairs from the attic. In the shadows, he could see the hidden panel open, and the outline of someone creeping into the room. Kip remained still and waited. When the intruder reached for the journal, Kip grabbed his hand and flashed a light into the surprised face of Silas McQuaide.

Kip's accusing eyes riveted the old man with guilt. McQuaide stood motionless, speechless, without explanation. His mouth twisted, trying to give an excuse, but there was none. He was caught red-handed, and he knew it.

"You've got a lot of explaining to do, McQuaide," Kip said, with cool authority.

McQuaide pulled from Kip's iron-like grip, and sank down into a chair. He put his hands to his head and whimpered, "Let's not be hasty. I was just playing a little joke on Miz Tilford. I just wanted to scare her a little."

"And why is that? Why did you want to scare Maggie? You'd better come clean with me, McQuaide. You're one step away from being arrested. I assure you, I'll press charges for breaking and entering."

Beads of perspiration popped out on the old man's forehead, and his hands began to shake. "Now Cap'n, there's no need to do that. I'll explain."

"Before you begin, there's someone who needs to witness this." Kip picked up the phone and called Maggie. "We've caught our man, Maggie, and he has something to tell us."

Kip had barely hung up the phone when Maggie bolted into the room. McQuaide looked down at the floor, unable to face her cold stare, then without warning, he leaped from the chair, grabbed the journal and ran for the door. Kip tackled him, and as they struggled, the lining of the cover ripped open, and a folded piece of paper fell to the floor. Maggie snatched the paper as Kip retrieved the journal, and threw McQuaide back into the chair.

Maggie sat on the edge of the bed, staring in disbelief at the paper in her hand. "Kip," she uttered, "it's the will, and it names Tabatha West as sole heir."

Silas McQuaide's eyes popped from their sockets, then he surrendered a long heavy sigh, and slumped to the floor—dead.

The death of Silas McQuaide left questions unanswered.

Who is Tabatha West?

Why is military paraphernalia in the attic?

What is Otto Von Kulow's connection with the jewels?

Where are the jewels now?

These questions and more plagued Kip. "There's one person who might have some answers," he said.

"Who's that?"

"Adele Merriman. Remember, she was once married to Otto."

"She probably doesn't know he's back in the country, Kip. How can she help?"

"Adele knows what went on during the war, and she may know about the jewels. She also knew the Hilliard family, and perhaps she knows Tabatha West. I say we pay Adele a visit."

Adele had just taken a fresh tin of muffins from the oven, and was setting them on a rack to cool when Kip and Maggie came into the bakery. She tried to mask her surprise with a forced smile.

"Hello, I assumed the two of you had gone back to Boston. How about a fresh Morning Glory muffin? I just took a batch from the oven."

"We didn't come for muffins today, Adele. We came to talk to you."

"Oh? What do you want to talk about?" Her expression grew tense and serious.

"What do you know about a family by the name of Hilliard, and a man named Otto Von Kulow?".

"Stop right there." Adele's voice turned sour and unfriendly. "I have nothing to say about any of them. You're prying into a personal matter, and you have no right."

"On the contrary, Adele, I have every right. You see, I've extended my stay on Nantucket because of Emily Hilliard. I was sent here to find her will, which I have located, and it names Tabatha West as the sole heir to the Hilliard estate."

"I still don't see how this concerns me."

"I'm trying to locate Tabatha West, and I hope you can help me. I recently discovered that a treasure of stolen jewels may be hidden somewhere on the estate, and a man by the name of Otto Von Kulow is involved."

Adele's expression reflected a "deer in the headlight" look. Her voice mellowed. She paused, and then said, "This will take a while. It's a long story." She hung an **Out to Lunch** sign on the door, and then led them into a small sitting room off the kitchen.

She gave a deep sigh. "Where do you want me to begin?"

"Tell us about the Hilliard family."

Her eyes saddened as she began her story. "They were summer people who bought an old Victorian house off Brant Point. When they winterized the place, they began spending holidays there as well. They had one daughter whose name was Doria, and they became guardians of Joe Hilliard's second cousin Bridget McGlone, after her mother died of influenza. The girls were as close as sisters, and when they married they had a double wedding."

"According to the Joe Hilliard's journal, Bridget married your son Karl."

Adele breathed another long sigh. "Yes, Bridget married my little Karl." The mention of her son's name brought tears to the old woman's eyes. Kip gave her time to compose herself before pressing on.

"Karl and I weren't close because he was taken from me by his father…"

"Otto Von Kulow." Maggie interjected.

"Yes and the mere mention of his name makes me ill. He was a horrible husband, but a good father to Karl."

"We believe Otto is back in this country, and has been for some time." Maggie said.

"Oh dear me, no," Adele groaned. "Why would he dare come back?"

"He and Silas McQuaide are convinced there's a stash of jewels hidden at the Hilliard estate. We have evidence that your husband has been living as a hermit on Tuckernuck for the past ten years, and visits the old house frequently in search of the jewels," Kip said.

"Those two have been up to no good since the Great War. They supplied food and clothing to German spies who entered the country. The house that Silas later converted into an inn had a secret room. That's where the Germans stayed until they could get to the mainland. Silas used his fishing boat under the cover of darkness to transport the men from the U-boats to the island. Otto and Silas were never caught, but people had a strong suspicion, and that's why Otto left right after the Armistice was signed in 1918, and he took little Karl with him. Silas maintained a low profile until the outbreak of WWII, then he started his subversive activities again. This time the U-boats delivered the saboteurs to the beach in inflatable boats. Fortunately many were caught before they reached the safe house, thanks to the vigilance of the coast watchers."

"That explains the military clothing and the German machine gun Maggie and I found in the secret room." Then Kip asked, "What about Tabatha West?"

"She must have been Emily's granddaughter. Doria's married name was West. I recall Emily and two little girls visiting my bakery oftentimes. I never knew their names, but they were cute little things, both had blond hair. Emily adored them. She always bought them a treat, and it was the same each time—a beach plum donut with cream cheese icing. I made those donuts especially for those two little girls, but after the accident—" Her voice cracked, unable to continue.

There was an awkward pause, and the room fell silent. Adele had a sad faraway look in her eyes. She took a handkerchief from her apron pocket, and dabbed away the tears. It was apparent the woman was unable to go on.

"Adele," Kip said with compassion, "you've given us a lot of important information today. I want to continue this session at another time. May we come back tomorrow?"

"I suppose so, Kip. I've held this inside for too long. Maybe it's time the truth be known, and if it will help find Emily's granddaughter, then it will be worth it."

"By the way, Adele," Kip added, "you might be interested to know that Silas McQuaide dropped dead of a heart attack a short time ago."

A broad smile spread across the woman's face. She said nothing, but the smile said it all.

After the death of Silas McQuaide the inn closed, and Maggie and Kip moved to the Gordon Folger Hotel. That evening they had dinner in the hotel dining room. The hotel was located at the bottom of Brant Point. It was once a grand place where affluent New Yorkers and Bostonians vacationed each summer. Its original name had been the Point Breeze, so named because of the balmy sea breezes that blew across its porches on summer nights. After a fire in 1925 destroyed half of the structure, the hotel closed its doors and remained closed until it was sold at auction in 1933. In 1936, it reopened under a new name; the Gordon Folger. It was a stately old building, typical Nantucket architecture; fog gray with white trim.

Maggie and Kip ordered a lobster salad with a glass of Zinfandel. This was a special evening. Having found the Hilliard will, Kip could focus on Maggie's case, which—hopefully—would reveal her as the lost heir, Tabatha West.

"I believe we are about to uncover who you are, Maggie," said Kip.

She looked across the table at him. The candlelight reflected sadness in her eyes.

"What's wrong? This is why you came here in the first place. You should be overjoyed."

"Perhaps, but I'm not. I'm afraid."

"What are you afraid of?"

"I'm afraid of what I might discover. Maybe you were right. Perhaps I should leave well enough alone."

"It's too late to back out now. We have to find out

if you're Tabatha West, for Emily's sake. Of course, there's a chance that you aren't. If not, then you can call the whole thing off, go back to Indiana, and remain Maggie Tilford for the rest of your life. However, before you do that, we're going to follow this through to the end. Is that clear?"

"I suppose you're right, but remember if it proves that I'm not Emily Hilliard's granddaughter, I'm dropping the case."

"That's fair enough," he agreed. Then he added, "I want to take another look at the photos included with your adoption papers. Perhaps now, they will make more sense."

When they returned to Maggie's room, she reached into the brown envelope containing the adoption papers and took out the photos. The first photo was of the two little girls on the beach. In the second picture, one girl was holding a rag doll. In the third photo the two sat on a stone bench near a tree. In the remaining photo were the same girls with a middle-age woman. On the back of that photo was the inscription, *Nan and girls, Summer 1942.*

"It's clear now," Kip said, "the woman in the photo is Emily. One girl is Tabatha, and the other is Bridget's child, but which is which?"

"There's a chance that Bridget is my mother instead of Dorie," Maggie said, toying with the gold heart-shape necklace around her neck.

"That's a possibility. Did Bridget's girl stay home that day, or did Tabatha?"

The next afternoon Kip and Maggie returned to Adele's bakery.

"Thank you for talking with us again, Adele," Kip said kindly.

A pot of fresh brewed tea and blueberry muffins had been prepared for them in the sitting room of Adele's bakeshop. She placed a **Closed** sign on the front door and pulled the shade.

"Where did I leave off yesterday?" she asked wearily.

"You mentioned little girls and the beach plum donuts," Maggie reminded her.

"Oh, yes. They were both sweet little girls, but one in particular stole my heart. She was a dear little thing. Both girls were blond, but one had lighter hair than the other, and there was something special about her. You reminded me of her, Maggie, when Kip brought you into my bakeshop that first day, and when you asked for a beach plum donut, I almost fainted. It was like she had come back to me."

"I apologize for that, Adele. I have no idea why I made such a request. As I told you, I've never heard of a beach plum."

"Never mind, child. You had no way of knowing."

"You mentioned earlier, that something caused you to stop baking those donuts. What happened?" Maggie asked.

"It was an awful tragedy. It happened on the July 4, 1942. I remember it as though it was yesterday. It started out to be a beautiful day, gentle breeze, just right for sailing. Dorie and her husband, along with Bridget, and…." her voice cracked.

Maggie put her arm around the old woman attempting to comfort her.

Adele put her hand up. "It's all right," she said, regaining her composure. "My son Karl died with them that day. We were not close after his father took him back to Germany, but he was still my little Karl, and I loved him."

"There was a child with them that day. Do you know who she was?" Kip asked.

"No, I don't. Emily never came to my bakery again. I don't know which child died, but I couldn't bring myself to make the beach plum donuts again."

"Has Otto tried to contact you?"

"Of course not," Adele spouted. "If he does, I will turn him in to the authorities. I protected him once, but that was a mistake. Money doesn't make up for the loss of a child. He paid me to keep silent and promised he would bring Karl back after one year, but he didn't. I was foolish to trust him."

Kip leaned forward in his chair, lowered his voice, and asked, "Do you know if Karl was involved with spy activity and smuggling during WWII?"

Adele hung her head in shame. "I suspect he was. I think he followed his father's example. I believe he and Silas McQuaide transported and protected men from the U-boats, whose intent was to sabotage defense plants on the mainland."

"What makes you think so?" Kip asked.

"I was on the beach one night coast watching when I heard voices near the shore. I crept close enough to overhear Karl's voice telling the men to follow him to a safe place."

"The Seafarers Inn?"

"Yes. But before they left, one man handed Karl a small pouch," Adele said.

"Do you know what was in the pouch?"

"No, but I'm certain it was payment for his services."

"Why didn't you report the incident to the Coast Guard?"

"I wouldn't betray my own son, don't you see. I kept silent after his death to protect his name—and mine. I didn't want people to associate his misdeeds with those of his father."

"Did McQuaide continue aiding the Germans after Karl's death?"

"I don't know, and I don't care."

After returning to the hotel, Kip sat back in his chair digesting all that Adele had told them. He put his hand to his chin, pondering. "I wonder if the pouch Karl received that night contained the jewels, and he hid them somewhere on the Hilliard property. They would be safe there, and he could retrieve them after the war and return to Germany."

"That explains why Otto returned. With Karl dead, and the jewels remained on Nantucket, and he had to come back to get them," said Maggie. "And to stay out of sight, he took up residence on Tuckernuck. McQuaide supplied him with food during the summer and allowed him to hide in the attic during the winter. That explains the reason for the blanket and mattress left the secret room."

"And that's why McQuaide invented the ghost story. If guests heard noises coming from the attic, they would assume it was the ghost of Captain Braddock." A satisfied look spread over Kip's face. "Finally the pieces of the puzzle are beginning to come together."

"Except for one," Maggie said sadly. "We don't know if Tabatha West was the little girl who drowned that day, or if it was the other child."

"Maggie, we have to go back to the old house. It's trying to tell you something, and you have to find out what it is."

"Kip, I'm so afraid."

"You have to go. It's the only way."

A spirit of sadness hovered over the old house. Through the gloom, a voice whispered to Maggie, pulling her inside.

She took a step forward. "Let's get this over with," she said with teeth clinched.

They entered the house, walked slowly across the foyer, then up the stairs to the nursery. The moment she crossed the threshold, Maggie felt a sense of sorrow weighing her down, causing a heaviness in her chest.

She took the rag doll from the carriage and held it

close. Familiar, long ago images focused in her mind, tortured recollections that had been buried for years. Her face flushed with emotion, and there was a distant look in her eyes as the memories surfaced.

"We were going sailing that day, but I got sick and stayed behind. The little girl left Raggedy Maggie with me for company. She said she would see me when she got back. I watched from here," Maggie said, walking to the window. *"I waved good-bye. I watched the boat until it disappeared, then I went to bed and took a long nap. When I awakened they hadn't returned, so I went downstairs and sat on her lap."*

"Whose lap, Maggie?" Kip whispered.

"Her lap. The woman in the painting. She held me, and I began to cry. She told me that everything would be all right." Maggie's voice began to crack with tears.

"Keep going, Maggie. What happened next?"

"It was getting dark, and the lady began to worry. She took me by the hand and we went down by the shore and looked for them, but they weren't there. They never came home."

"Who? Who never came home?"

"Mommy and Daddy. They never came home!" she screamed. Her entire body reeled with remorse.

Kip waited until she calmed down, then he prompted her to continue. "What happened next?"

She stood mute for a moment, then subconscious thoughts began to surface again. *"A terrible storm came. The wind began to blow very hard. I could hear the wind chimes in the garden ringing in my ears. We ran back to the house and waited. A man came and held the woman and me in his arms. We all were crying. The man kept repeating, 'Dorie, Dorie.' "*

"Do you know the man's name?"

"The woman called him—Joe."

"What else happened?"

"We waited for a long time. It got very dark, and I fell asleep. When I woke up, the woman told me that my mommy and daddy weren't coming home. I don't remember anything after that."

She dropped the doll and closed her eyes, sobbing. Finally, she was at peace with herself and with the house. This had been her home. The old house had been trying to tell her that. It had wooed her, and it had won her back.

The puzzle was almost complete. There was no doubt she was one of the little girls mentioned in Professor Hilliard's journal, but was she Tabatha West?

Chapter 25

Emily

*B*oston's Logan Airport was a tangled mass of people rushing in all directions to meet flight schedules. Kip and Maggie managed to push their way through the crowd, then they hailed a cab to Kip's office.

J.P. Witherspoon was waiting for them when they arrived. "Kip, my boy. It's good to see you again, and who's this lovely lady with you?"

"J.P. I'd like you to meet my client, Maggie Tilford."

The elder attorney gave Maggie a long look. "You look familiar," he said, "have we met before?"

"Yes, briefly. I scheduled an appointment with you earlier, but you were unable to see me because of an emergency, that's when Mr. Kippington took my case."

"I apologize for that, my dear, but you're in good hands with Mr. Kippington."

Maggie winked at Kip. "Yes," she agreed, "very good hands."

"You see, Sir," Kip began, "in the process of searching for the Hilliard will, we stumbled on some strong evidence regarding Miss Tilford's case as well. I believe they coincide."

"Oh? How's that?"

"Well, Maggie—Miss Tilford came here in search of her birth parents. Apparently, you handled the case years ago."

"Tilford? I don't recall that name."

"But your signature was on the letters from your office dated 1943," Maggie insisted.

"That was my father. He retired in 1945 and has since passed, God rest his soul."

Maggie was dismayed. "Then if Mr. Kippington hadn't taken my case, my trip to Boston would have been wasted."

"I'm afraid so," the elder man agreed.

"It was fate," Kip said. "Had you not been called out of town to see Emily Hilliard, Maggie and I wouldn't have gone to Nantucket and discovered her birth family."

"What do you mean, Kip?"

"Well, while I was searching for Emily's will, Maggie was doing some snooping on her own. As it turned out our paths met in the middle. We have evidence that Maggie is part of the Hilliard family, but we aren't certain if she is the missing heir we're looking for."

"We were hoping you could give us some answers, but since you didn't handle Maggie's adoption—"

Witherspoon was taken back by the new revelation. "I don't have the answer, but perhaps Emily does. As I told you, Kip, Emily's mental condition has improved greatly, and seeing you, Maggie, might jog her memory."

"I'm not sure if I'm ready for this," she confessed.

"Nonsense. You'll be fine," Kip assured. "We'll learn once-and-for-all if you are Tabatha West."

"What if I'm Tabatha, but she doesn't recognize me?"

"That's the chance we'll have to take," Kip said.

"According to Emily's doctor, she's beginning to recall events from the past that have been blocked for years," Witherspoon remarked. "I'll phone the nursing home and alert them of our visit."

The Fairhaven nursing home was a large two-story brick Colonial that had once been a private residence, but was later converted into a mental facility for the elderly. It was a stately edifice, surrounded by a high wrought iron fence, framing a perfectly manicured lawn, filled with purple hydrangeas and tall shade trees.

Maggie sat in the back seat of Witherspoon's luxury Sudan, trying to calm the butterflies in her stomach as they drove through the gate, slowly following the circle drive leading to the main entrance.

Kip helped Maggie out of the car, giving her a reassuring smile. "Here we are."

"Yes," she sighed, "here we are." She tried to conceal her anxiety, but her stomach continued churn, and her heart pounded in her chest. "I'm really scared," she gasped, shivering with panic.

"Just remember," he told her, "whatever happens, I'll be here."

With Kip's encouraging words repeating in her mind, she took his arm and they climbed the steps leading to the front door. Witherspoon had gone ahead to inform the staff of their arrival, and he was waiting for Kip and Maggie in the foyer. The party was greeted by a prim woman in her late 50s.

"We've been expecting you, Mr. Witherspoon. My name is Sarah Rosen."

"Ms. Rosen, how nice to meet you. This is my associate, Dan Kippington, and Maggie Tilford."

"How nice to meet you," she smiled. "Please have a seat. I'll tell Dr. Riddell you're here."

In a short time, a tall distinguished-looking man walked into the room, wearing a casual sport coat with tan trousers. His button-down shirt was open at the collar exposing a colorful silk scarf around his neck. His hair was gray at the temples, giving the appearance of a college professor instead of a doctor. The three stood when he entered.

The doctor extended his hand. "It's good to see you again, Mr. Witherspoon. And who are your friends?"

"The young man is my associate, Dan Kippington, and the young lady is Maggie Tilford, who we suspect to be part of Emily's family."

Kip and Maggie shook hands with the doctor. "Pleased to meet you, Doctor," Kip said.

Maggie smiled, but remained silent. Her tongue felt like it was glued to the roof of her mouth.

"Please, sit down," the doctor said. "Let me tell you about Miss Emily before you visit her." He leaned back in his chair, crossed his legs, and lit his pipe. He took a puff, exhaled, then said, "I was pleased to hear that you found Miss Emily's will, and if you are her granddaughter," he said, addressing Maggie, "you'll make her last days very happy. Allow me to bring you up-to-speed on her case."

Maggie and Kip were on the edge of their seats waiting to hear what the doctor had to say.

"Emily Hilliard was admitted in December 1942, not long after her daughter and son-in-law were drowned in a boating accident."

"It is my understanding that another couple, Bridget and Karl Von Kulow along with a little girl were also drowned," Kip interjected.

"That's correct," agreed the doctor. "Bridget was a second cousin by marriage. Karl was her husband."

"Which little girl drowned," Maggie asked.

"Only Emily can answer that."

Dr. Riddell continued. "After the accident, Professor and Mrs. Hilliard were given sole custody of the surviving girl. They left Nantucket, and returned to

Boston. In the fall of that same year, tragedy struck again when the Professor was killed in an auto accident while driving to work."

Maggie let out a gasp. "Oh poor Emily. No wonder she had a nervous breakdown."

"It was far more serious than that. She had a total mental collapse. She lost all sense of the past, buried it into her subconscious, and that's where it has been all these years—until recently."

"What happened to the child after Emily was committed?" Kip asked.

"Emily's condition appeared hopeless. She was no longer able to care for the child, so the little girl became a ward of the court, and was put out for adoption. There was concern that she might not be adoptable due to the trauma of losing her parents, and the fact that she was not an infant. It's more difficult to find parents for older children."

"Did the girl speak of her parents after the accident?" Witherspoon inquired.

"Her mind went blank the day her parents died, and the events leading up to the accident, as well. In other words, her life began at the time of her adoption. The couple who adopted her assumed a big responsibility, considering her mental state, and it remained uncertain whether she would ever remember the past."

"The Tilfords were wonderful people," Maggie said, her face sober, musing on fond memories.

"Doctor, exactly in what state is Miss Emily at present?" Witherspoon asked.

"As I stated earlier, Miss Emily came to her senses a few weeks ago, but she still fades in and out of reality. She mentioned the will and an heir. She's anxious to get her affairs in order."

The doctor stood to his feet, tapped his pipe and stuffed it back into the pocket of his sport coat. "With that said, are you ready to see Mrs. Hilliard?"

The three rose slowly from their seats, and—with overwhelming anticipation—they followed Dr. Riddell down the hallway, and through the double doors opening out into the garden. They paused, for a moment, as they stood on the brick patio overlooking a rose-covered gazebo. Sitting alone with her back to them was and elderly woman.

"Is that–?"

"Yes, Miss Tilford. That's Emily Hilliard."

Maggie looked up at Kip for reassurance.

"It's okay. You'll be fine. I'm here."

Maggie felt glued to the spot, unable to move forward. She looked at Kip for encouragement, and his smile gave her the strength to began her journey. The walk seemed endless, and the only thing that kept her going was the realization that each step brought her closer to the truth. She paused half-way, took a deep breath, and continued on until she reached her destination.

"Miss Emily," Maggie whispered.

The woman didn't respond.

Maggie repeated a little louder, "Miss Emily."

The woman stirred in her chair. Out of the stillness,

came a frail voice, "Who are you? Step closer so that I can see you."

Maggie felt as though her heart would explode, and her knees began to buckle.

Emily Hilliard's face reflected years of sadness. It was difficult to recognize her as the same woman in the painting. Her face was weathered with wrinkles, and her beautiful chestnut hair had turned white. Her eyes, however, though clouded with age, remained soft and gentle. She sat straight in her chair with her frail hands folded in her lap. Her hair was fashioned in a prim bun atop her head. Her dress was black, with long sleeves trimmed in delicate white lace.

Emily stared at Maggie, straining to get a clear view. "I don't have many visitors," she said in a cracked voice. "Do I know you?"

"I'm not sure if you do or not." Maggie's heart sank. *Suppose Emily didn't recognize her. Suppose she wasn't Tabatha West, after all.*

A gentle breeze rustled the wind chimes hanging from the center of the gazebo.

The old woman's eyes lit up. A note of pleasure filled her voice. "The wind chimes make beautiful music. My husband made wind chimes years ago. It was his hobby. The doctor allowed me bring a set with me, and he hung them here for my enjoyment."

"They are lovely," Maggie agreed.

"The wind chimes remind me of Joe's love. We had them hanging on the porch of our home on Nantucket. I loved listening to them on summer nights. Sometimes Joe left notes for me hidden in one of the metal tubes."

"That sounds very romantic," Maggie smiled. "Tell me about your summer house."

There was a supernatural glow in Emily's eyes. "It was a grand house. It was filled with love, and we had many good times there—Joe, Dorie, Bridget and I. Dorie was our daughter and Bridget was our cousin. When Bridget's mother died, we raised her as our own."

"Where are they now?" Maggie realized this was a cruel question, but she hoped it would jog Emily's memory.

"Dead. They're all dead. Aren't the wind chimes lovely. Joe made them. It was his hobby." Tears welled up in her eyes.

Maggie touched the woman's hand. "Miss Emily, tell me about Dorie."

She lifted her eyes to Maggie. The reflection of the painful memories were evident.

"I told Joe the boat wasn't safe. It needed repair, but he insisted is was sea worthy. Dorie loved the sea, and the sea killed her. Oh Dorie, Dorie, my sweet daughter," she uttered in a ghostly moan.

"How did Dorie die? Miss Emily."

She thought for a moment, closed her eyes, and then took a deep breath. "It was in July, I think. They had all gone sailing. Joe and I stayed behind with Eva. It began to get dark, so Eva and I went to the beach to watch for them. We saw a storm blowing over the water. The waves were high, and deadly. The boat capsized and they were all drowned."

"Miss Emily, you mentioned the little girl on the beach with you that day. What was her name again?

"Eva. Bridget's little girl."

Maggie's heart sank. "Are you sure her name was Eva—not Tabatha?"

"Tabatha? Who is Tabatha?"

"Tabatha was your granddaughter, Dorie and Jamison's child."

"Oh, yes. You are right. I did have a granddaughter by that name, but she died with the rest."

Emily looked hard at Maggie. Her eyes widened. "I think I know you," she beamed, leaning forward in her chair to get a better look. As she did so, her eyes fell upon the gold heart-shaped necklace around Maggie's neck. "Tabby! You're Tabby. Eva didn't stay behind. It was you. I've been so confused. I thought you died that day."

She held out her arms and Maggie sank into her embrace, both sobbing tears of joy. Maggie hadn't been aware of the tremendous amount of pressure that had built up over the past weeks, until it was finally released. Her decisive moment had arrived.

"Are you sure that I'm Tabatha?"

Emily's eyes were bright and clear. "I'm very sure, my dear. You're wearing the locket. I thought you looked familiar when I first saw you, but I couldn't place you until I noticed the locket."

"This locket was with my adoption papers," Maggie said.

"The locket belonged to Eva's mother, it was a gift from her mother Molly, and Bridget gave it to her daughter Eva."

"Then why do *I* have it?" Maggie questioned.

"We were gathering Eva's belongings after the accident, and the locket was among her things. I gave the locket to you, because you and Eva were so close. I felt she would want you to have it. There's a tiny catch at the bottom. If you open it, you will see the initials BMG. That stands for Bridget McGlone. Her mother had those initials engraved on the locket. It was Molly's legacy to her daughter."

Emily placed her hand on her granddaughter's head and stroked it lovingly. "I love the sound of wind chimes, don't you? Joe made them for me." Gradually the woman's eyes grew dim. She was drifting back. "I'm tired. I must rest now."

"I'll come back and visit again, Grandmother."

The woman looked at her through glazed eyes. "Do I know you?" Reality had slipped through the windows of her mind, but this time peace mirrored in her eyes.

"We've lost her again," Dr. Riddell said sadly. "But for a few moments she recognized you."

"Will she remember my visit?" Maggie asked.

"I can't promise that she will, but it's possible she might. And if she does remember your visit today, it will make her very happy," the doctor assured.

Maggie fell into Kip's arms. "Oh, Kip," she cried, "I found Emily and lost her in the same day."

"Perhaps you have lost Emily, but you have found Tabatha." He kissed her gently on the forehead. "Come on," he said, "let's get back to Nantucket."

Chapter 26

The Puzzle Is Complete

Maggie rose early the next morning and walked down to the beach. As she sat quietly on a large flat rock at the foot of the lighthouse, she pondered the events that had transpired since her arrival on Nantucket. She had accomplished what she had set out to do—find her identy. Unfortunately, Maggie's only living relative, Emily Hilliard, was mentally unstable and might not remember their reunion.

A short distance away was Steamboat Wharf, reminding her that she would soon leave Nantucket…and Kip. A stabbing pain came to her heart at the thought of not seeing him again. Without Kip's support, she lacked the courage pursue the truth. Dan Kippington was her tower of strength, and she didn't want lose him.

Maggie had no plans to return to Nantucket. Now that she knew who her family had been and how they died, she wanted to leave the past behind. As far as the

old house was concerned, once it was in her posses-
sion, she would sell it.

She got up and walked further down the beach,
stopping occasionally to watch the friendly surf tumble
lazily inland. A flock of seagulls circled overhead,
screeching in the wind, while the hollow sound of
the buoy clanked in the distance. The sky was clear,
and the water calm. She bent down and picked up
a periwinkle shell, dropped it into her pocket, then
headed back to town.

The twisted streets and lanes of Nantucket had
no planned direction, but instead wondered at their
own will like winding brooks. Picket fences enclosed
secluded back yard gardens, where sweet-scented
flowers grew in abundance. The island was a special
place, and she would miss it.

As Maggie wound her way back to the Gordon
Folger, she was reminded that, in some ways,
Nantucket hadn't changed over the years. Of course,
the steely blow of the blacksmith's hammer could no
longer be heard on the wharves, nor the sound of the
casks as they rolled over wooden docks. Gone too,
was the creaking sound of the whale ship's tackle, and
the shouts of the whalers preparing to sail. Never the
less, the spirit of old Nantucket managed to survive.
Nantucket Island was a step back in time, and she
hoped it would always remain so. It was strange how
the little patch of sand, just thirty miles off the coast
of Cape Cod, had altered her life, and she would carry
away its charm—magic—in her heart forever.

"I've several things to sort through," Maggie told Kip. "I'm not sure where Tabatha West fits into my life. Perhaps she doesn't fit in at all. Maybe just knowing the truth is enough."

"Don't forget the summer house will be yours, Maggie. You must consider it in your future plans."

"I don't want it," she said decidedly. "There are too many ghosts...I mean memories there."

"But some of those memories were happy ones," he reminded her.

"Perhaps so, but they're so vague that I can hardly remember. However, I would like to make one more visit to the house before I leave the island. Will you go with me, Kip?"

"Of course," he smiled, taking her by the hand. "Let's go."

There was little conversation between them as they strolled down the beach. The steady roll of the surf splashing against the shore echoed around them, while plucky little sandpipers darted in front of them, scavenging for food washed in by the sea.

The house waited for Maggie—as it had for years. A renewed admiration for the old place fell over her. "It's a shame to let such a lovely old house die away," she sighed.

"You could make it live again," Kip told her.

"Maybe," she replied.

Kip followed Maggie as she walked up the rickety porch steps. The front door squeaked as she opened it. Maggie stood at the threshold, where her attention was drawn again to the painting in the parlor. She paused—deep in thought. She remembered the kindness in Emily's eyes when she recognized her as her missing granddaughter. That same kindness was portrayed in the painting.

The gallery of family photos was still missing from the upstairs hallway. "I wonder what happened to them." Maggie commented.

"Silas McQuaide probably took them. More than likely, he stashed them away at the inn. The new owner may come across them sometime."

"Why would he take them in the first place?" Maggie asked.

"It was just another way of spooking you. He would have tried anything to scare you away," Kip replied.

Maggie's lips curled in anger. "Well, it backfired. As it turned out, he's the one whose gone—permanently."

Maggie paused at the door of the nursery. "There's one thing McQuaide overlooked," she quipped.

"What's that?"

"Raggedy Maggie. I'm going to take her with me. Eva left her in my care many years ago. Having the doll is like having part of Eva with me."

When they revisited the garden, Maggie imagined how beautiful it must have been, as she visualized it in the stillness of her mind. "Eva and I played here, under the oak tree. I wonder what my life would have been, if it hadn't stormed that day."

"That's something you'll never know," Kip told her. "One thing for sure, we would have never met."

Maggie looked into his eyes. "That's true," she agreed. "We wouldn't have met."

Kip seized the moment. Gathering her in his arms, he whispered, "This doesn't have to be the end for *us*, you know." His lips touched hers like a whisper, soft, gentle, sensual. Maggie felt safe in his strong arms. The pain from the past melted away, and she was ready to face the future with new hope and a new relationship.

A soft breath of air stirred the wind chimes. They made a happy melody that was carried on the breeze throughout the garden. Maggie glanced up at them.

"Grandfather Hilliard made those," she said. It was a hobby of his. Grandmother Hilliard told me he sometimes slipped a love note in one of the metal tubes. Kip, would you take the wind chimes down for me. I want to take them along too."

When Kip removed the wind chimes, he noticed something sticking out of one of the hollow cylinders. When he pulled it out, he discovered a small rolled-up piece of paper with writing on it. He handed it to Maggie.

When she unrolled it up, she realized it was, in fact, a note from Joe.

> *Dearest Girl*
> *Always remember this is your home. It is*
> *filled with love.*
> *Keep it. Cherish it. Never let it go.*
> *Love,*
> *Joe*

A telephone message from J.P. Witherspoon was waiting for Kip when they arrived back at the Gordon Folger. After taking the message, Kip's eyes filled with sorrow. "Maggie," he said, "I'm afraid I have some sad news. Emily Hilliard died peacefully this morning. Her last words were, 'Tabby's home'."

A flash of grief ripped through her. Her voice broke. "She remembered me," she whispered, and then she slumped into a nearby chair and wept.

They booked passage on the late ferry for Hyannis, but before leaving, they wanted to say good-bye to Adele Merriman, and inform her that the little girl who died in the accident was her granddaughter, Eva.

The weekend tourists crowded the streets of downtown Nantucket. The harbor was filled with sailing craft ranging in size from sailboats to luxury yachts. The dinner crowd formed long lines outside the eateries waiting to be admitted. Several customers were in the bakery when Kip and Maggie arrived. They discretely waited until the shop was empty before they approached Adele.

"Kip! Maggie!" She greeted them with a smile.

"We're leaving on the evening ferry, and we've come to say good-bye, Adele."

"Will you be returning this summer,?" she asked.

"Perhaps." Kip replied. "Maggie has some unfinished business here, and I may accompany her."

"Thank you, for your cooperation the other day. The information was most helpful," Maggie told her.

"Maggie was able to talk to Emily Hilliard before she died," Kip said, "and Emily identified her as Tabatha West, her granddaughter."

"Who was the other little girl?" Adele asked. Her voice was thin and strained.

Maggie touched the older woman's hand. Her sympathetic look told Adele what she had suspected all along.

"She was my granddaughter, wasn't she."

"Yes, Adele, I'm afraid she was. Her name was Eva. Eva Von Kulow."

Adele slumped forward and put her hands on the counter to keep her balance. "They never told me who she was, but I knew. She had Karl's features. How I loved that little girl." Adele's eyes began to swim.

Maggie unfastened the gold heart-shaped necklace from around her neck and pressed it into the older woman's hand. "This was hers," she said. "I want you to have it as a keepsake."

Adele held the necklace as though it was worth a fortune. "Thank you," she managed to say, wiping away her tears with the edge of her apron.

When Maggie and Kip turned to leave, Adele called out, "Wait! Maggie, I have something for you." She handed her a small, white paper bag. Inside was a beach plum donut with cream cheese icing.

It was dusk. The sun hung low like a brass lamp in the sky. Maggie stood on the top deck of the *Nobska*, taking one last look at the island, absorbing its beauty and charm. She was torn between wanting to stay and wanting to leave, and the two emotions waged a war within her. Hot tears began to trickle down her face.

Kip slipped his arm around her waist.

"I'm going to miss the Grey Lady," she cried. "I didn't realize how much I've come to love this island."

"It's the magic," Kip smiled, "Remember, I warned you about Nantucket's power of enchantment."

She smiled through her tears. "Yes," she agreed, "and I said that would never happen to me—but it has. Yet, in spite of all that has happened, I'm not sure if I'll be able to return."

The Nobska's powerful engine groaned, and the ferry gave a jolt as it backed out of the slip. Kip placed two pennies into the palm of Maggie's hand. "There's an old saying," he told her, "that if you toss two pennies over the side of the ferry as you pass Brant Point, someday you'll return. You make your choice, but whichever you decide, I hope this is just the beginning for us. It's your decision."

Kip joined the other passengers, leaving Maggie alone with her thoughts.

The ferry resounded a departing signal and backed away from the dock making its way to Brant Point. Maggie looked longingly at the island. Silently she said good-bye to the gray-shingle houses, the picket fences, the rose-covered cottages, the lighthouses, the church spires, and all the things that made Nantucket a special place. How could she *not* come back! Through her tears, she waited for the steamer to pass Brant

Point Light. When the Nobska eased by the lighthouse, she dropped the two pennies overboard and watched as they disappeared beneath the surface of the water.

Maggie stood alone until Nantucket became a thin gray strip on the horizon, then she joined Kip and the others. As she sat down beside him, she placed her empty hand in his.

His face lit up with a smile. "I love you," he said.

"And I love you, my darling."

The rag doll lying in Maggie's lap had a big smile painted on its face because it knew a secret. A little black bag was stuffed inside the doll's body, and in that bag, were the missing jewels.

Epilogue

Maggie returned to Indiana. She contributed a monetary gift from the sale of the farm to the Baptist Church where Jim and Margaret Tilford had been lifelong members. She and Kip were married a year later, and made their home in Boston. They maintained the house on Nantucket as a summer home, and moved there permanently after Kip retired. They had one daughter—Emily. Maggie never changed her name to Tabatha out of respect for Jim and Margaret Tilford, whom she considered her *real* parents.

Adele Merriman resumed making the beach plum donuts, which became very popular with the locals and visitors alike. She died peacefully in her sleep in 1965. She was wearing the gold heart-shaped necklace at the time of her death.

When Otto Von Kulow learned about the death of Silas McQuaide, he gave up the search for the missing jewels and fled back to Germany. He died a bitter, lonely old man at the age of ninety-five.

The old house was refurbished with the remainder of the money received from her inheritance from the Tilford estate. Maggie honored her grandfather's wishes. She considered the old house her home and she cherished it until the day she died. The house was passed down to Kip and Maggie's daughter Emily, and she is living there today still carrying on the family tradition.

The Seafarers Inn was sold to a businessman from West Hartford, Connecticut. During the renovation, the photos taken from the Hilliard house were discovered in the basement of the inn. They were returned to Maggie, and they resumed their rightful place hanging in the upstairs hallway of the old house.

Herman the cat adjusted to city life in Boston, and discovered that canned shrimp and tuna could not hold a candle to fresh fish from the ocean. He grew fat and happy, living to the ripe old age of twenty-three.

And as for Raggedy Maggie, well—as far as I know— she has kept her secret all these years, and I suspect it will stay that way.

Printed in the United States
by Baker & Taylor Publisher Services